THE LEGEND OF
STOVEPIPE PEAT

HELEN R. LETTS

With gratitude to my family
Carol Choat and Patricia Jones
And to friends Heidi Schmitz,
Ingrid Smith, Laurie Correl,
and Angela Picarazzi

1

Celebrating A Community Tradition

ONCE A BUSTLING VILLAGE, CENTURIES LATER Principio Furnace was a bedroom community for people who worked in manufacturing and high-demand jobs in towns near and far. Still, the small community held on to traditions, and Hallowe'en was a welcome and much celebrated tradition in Principio Furnace.

Hallowe'en themed decorations adorned the porches and doors of the old bungalows made of stone and clapboard and tiny shops that framed the town square. It didn't matter that there was no official competition or prizes awarded for the best decorated or for the scariest or the creepiest decorations. It didn't dilute the ferocity by which neighbor battled neighbor for acclaim. Those who were fans and followers of social networking sites posted pictures of their Hallowe'en decorations and gleefully, like hungry sharks fed off the likes and comments.

Corn stalks that months earlier, ears removed, were wrapped with twine and hung to dry upside down from metal hooks, now were propped on porches and near doors up and down the streets. Rainbow colored Indian corn, husks stripped back, hung alongside the golden-colored stalks with the flowering male tassels intact. Plain, dried, and painted gourds were added to further promote the season, living beyond October 31st and into November.

Carving pumpkins, big ones, little ones, some tall and skinny, others round and fat, the rind shiny and orange, had been transformed into Hallowe'en jack-o'-lanterns. Many had been carved to look like the face of some grotesque or ghoulish monster, the silhouette of a cat with an exaggerated arched back, a trio of bats, or simply a toothy happy face with a nose and two eyes the shape of triangles. Bold warnings like Boo, Trick or Treat, and Beware were carved in thick lettering into the outer layer of the pumpkin. And for safety reasons alone, the jack-o'-lanterns were illuminated, not by burning wax candles, but by LED lights.

Residents who happily welcomed the arrival of fall and Hallowe'en artfully combined and stacked pumpkins. It wasn't unusual to see a squat French Cinderella pumpkin that inspired the fairytale angled alongside a Knucklehead pumpkin covered in the greenish bumps that looked like warts positioned next to a white Ghost pumpkin. Still others merely added Blue Doll, Pink, and Long Island Cheese pumpkins to their existing porch décor or placed as lone decorations on front steps.

Competition for creating the best front door decoration was as stiff as it was for designing the most eye-catching porch. Front doors became the backdrop for things like a three-dimensional skeleton or a giant cobweb made from stretched cotton balls populated with gigantic black spiders with yellow eyes. There was even a door that displayed the crafted frontal image of a long-nosed, pointy-eared green goblin with blood-red eyes and something brown, gnarly, and slimy hanging from its crooked teeth. There was no limit to people's imagination.

Witches' legs dressed in narrow-striped black and orange socks and ruby red shoes stuck out of bushes. Imitation black crows clung to the edge of cauldrons alongside witch brooms. Ghosts made from stiffened cheese cloth with black felt eyes hung from porch ceilings and the branches of Northern Red Oak, maple, and birch trees that grew throughout the town. Fake severed hands, large, hairy, and putrid green, gripped handrails. And the town's only market, Babe's Place, at the end of Main Street, and J.D.'s sub shop beside it featured windows with colorful hand-painted Hallowe'en scenes that attracted adults and children alike.

Mrs. Rittenhouse, a long-retired schoolteacher, strolled into the town square shortly before the festival was scheduled to begin. Barely five-foot two, she wore an old burlap bag with the words "Old Potato Sack" stitched in brown lettering across the back. Heart-shaped, three-dimensional green leaves made of felt connected by small pieces of dark brown twine, ran from front to back and across her torso. She directed her 17-year-old grandson, Ethan Harrington, and his friend, David Eckman, to retrieve folding tables from the bed of an old blue pickup truck. The boys, dressed in skeleton costumes designed to glow in the dark, set up the tables. Volunteers, all residents of Principio, all dressed in costumes, and under the direction of the formidable Mrs. Rittenhouse, moved in like a swarm of bees and covered the tables with black gingham tablecloths as they did every year.

By the time the festival was ready to begin, plates of homemade cookies in fun Hallowe'en shapes, pumpkin bread and frosted cupcakes, caramel apples, pumpkin bars, and slices of pumpkin pie were placed on the tables. Assorted pieces of candy were placed in small brown paper bags sealed closed with a single holiday sticker and stacked in red-colored peck wood baskets. Small red Winesap and bicolored Fuji apples also filled wood baskets. And one entire table was set aside for hand-pressed apple cider in a dozen 5-gallon glass dispensers with spigots.

Pumpkins, big and small, and bales of hay from a generous farmer whose daughter and grandchildren called Principio Furnace home were staged throughout the square and very near the table claimed by Ethan and David to set up a laptop connected to portable Bluetooth speakers. The boys would be streaming spooky, creepy, and creaky Hallowe'en sounds and music to set the mood for trick or treaters.

At his grandmother's insistence, Bobby Pickett's *Monster Mash* would be at the top of the play list. Behind his gray-haired grandmother's back, Ethan and David had rolled their eyes when she demanded that Sheb Wooley's *The Purple People Eater* follow the 1962 song by Pickett and the Crypt-Kickers. And they barely stifled their groans when she wanted *The Addams Family Theme* by Vic Mizzy and Bette Midler belting out *I Put a Spell on You* from the Disney movie *Hocus Pocus* to complete the playlist. Ethan and David, however, had their own thoughts about what music should close out the playlist and conspired to make Michael Jackson singing *Thriller* their final choice.

To make sure the town square was properly lighted, a tower light like those used to illuminate some sports fields at night had been brought in. It was set up behind where the best friends stood so one of them could flip the power switch as night fell.

Meanwhile six blocks away at 137 Red Toad Way, the last male descendent of one of Principio Furnace's founding families, Jacob Biddle and his wife Martha, were in a battle over Jacob's costume.

"No," declared Jacob, pointing to the red velvet waistcoat with brass buttons she held. "A true pirate would not dress like that."

"It works," Martha answered, who was dressed as a medieval barmaid.

"Didn't you ever watch the old swashbuckler movies as a kid? Johnny Depp in *Pirates of the Caribbean*? This is too flamboyant. I'm a farmer."

Martha stood, arms crossed. She wore several petticoats topped by a red skirt, one corner of which was tucked into a black sash and a black lace-up chemise over a white blouse with telescoping sleeves. She proclaimed, "Tonight you're a pirate!"

Seeing the flash of temper in her brown eyes and the firm set of her jaw, Jacob had made an effort to appease her. "How about I wrap a red scarf around my head, wear the white shirt with puffed sleeves, and cover it with that old tattered black vest that extends past my hips?"

When she didn't respond, he added, "I'll wear black jeans and that wide belt with the big silver-toned square buckle you bought. That'll work don't you think?"

Martha considered it and said, "Okay." And told

him to, "Put on those Robin Hood boots I purchased last year. The festival is about to begin."

Jacob hurriedly dressed and together he and Martha walked rapidly to the town square.

True to tradition, at precisely 5 o'clock on Hallowe'en, the square and surrounding streets filled with smiling adults and giggling children carrying trick or treat bags of varying shapes and sizes. The children, at least the ones whose faces were not hidden behind a mask, could be seen grinning widely, dancing, skipping, and jumping up and down.

Because it was an exceptionally soft night, no one wore coats. Jacob and Martha joined the tail end of the colorful parade of witches, ghosts, mummies, vampires, zombies, princesses, fairies, dinosaurs, and popular movie heroes that drew applause from everyone. One particularly creative person came as the mythical Headless Horseman and another as a far too realistic Frankenstein. Infants, cradled in the arms of parents, were dressed as pumpkins, bumblebees, ladybugs, and lion cubs. One baby was dressed as Sesame Street's Cookie Monster and another as Elmo.

For the next two hours, Jacob and Martha mingled, greeted people they had seen just days before at one of the Biddle Farm pumpkin patches and many they had not seen in some time. Principio Furnace was Jacob's birthplace. The only son of James and Eve Biddle, Jacob and Martha lived in a two-story brick house his great-grandfather had built. Although the young couple had updated some appliances and electrical wiring and plumbing, and modified parts of the ground floor, the beautiful craftsmanship of the interior primarily remained intact. A closet in the kitchen still showed where Jacob's parents had tracked his growth, recording in ink the year, his age, and his height.

The house to the south of them was occupied by Earl and Harriet Johnson and their three children, all boys. The house to the north was occupied by the Armour family, Francis and Anne, who had a daughter, Patricia. All the children had been friends. Jacob remembered climbing trees nearly year-round and running through the woods chasing imaginary villains. And on really hot summer days, he and the others had grabbed a thick heavy rope tied to the limb of an old oak tree to swing from the steep embankment along Principio Creek and leap into the center of the creek where it was eight feet deep.

Earl and Harriet, now in their sixties, still lived next door, but the three sons did not. Each moved out of the area after being graduated from high school and returned at the holidays, usually Thanksgiving and Christmas. If time permitted, they always visited the Biddle's and shared a glass of eggnog with some special spirits.

Steven, the youngest Johnson son and the one closest in age to Jacob, returned to the area. Now married and the father of two, he worked as a machinist three towns over. Patricia Armour took over the family home when her parents retired to Florida. She married a dentist named Clint Greyson, gave birth to fraternal twins, and launched a career as a state trooper.

Hand in hand, Jacob and Martha toured the decorated houses around the square, greeting the children that called out to him as the "pumpkin man." With great sincerity, Martha praised the creativity and imagination that inspired porch and door decorations and expressed unguarded shame that she had done nothing. It was 15-year-old Nikki who worked part-time at Babe's Market who overheard Martha and didn't hesitate to correct her.

"Mrs. Biddle," she called out when she heard Martha's remark. "My mom and I walked by your house yesterday. She really, really liked your simple design. I know Mom would love to have your large old wooden bucket filled with white chrysanthemums on our front porch. And those big, really big, pumpkins on the steps and the. . . wow . . . the wreath on your front door . . . the witch . . . is totally fun."

Martha reached out, squeezed Nikki's hand, and said, "Thank you." Jacob leaned in, hugged his wife, and whispered in her ear, "Told you."

When the tour of houses was complete, Jacob and Martha found themselves moving to the beat of Monster Mash as they strolled toward the tables to sample treats prepared by residents. Jacob eyed the plate of pumpkin bread, grabbed a napkin, and was reaching for a slice when a male voice behind him demanded, "What are you doing?"

Jacob turned to see who had spoken and smiled broadly when he came face to face with his childhood friend wearing a baseball uniform. "Steven," he said with a smile. They exchanged a one-armed hug and a slap on the back.

Steven Johnson stepped back, did a visual survey of Jacob from head to toe, and remarked, "Good grief, Jacob. You're still dressing as a pirate?"

Jacob scanned his memory and recalled that as a pre-teen he liked being a pirate at Hallowe'en. Laughing, he said, "Isn't there a photo somewhere of BOTH of us as pirates?"

"There is," answered Steven. "Mom pulled it out earlier today to show my children. My daughter, Abby, thought it was very funny. Aaron's too young to care."

"And by the way," added Steven, pointing to the slices of bread, "That's Mom's pumpkin bread."

"Thought so," said Jacob, turning back to grab a slice. "The thick cream cheese icing with the crushed walnuts on top is the giveaway." He paused, took a bite, and said, "Yep. Your Mom makes the best pumpkin bread in Principio."

Martha joined Jacob, said hello to Steven and his wife Carol, who was dressed as a chef. She helped herself to a slice of pumpkin bread, repeating Jacob's opinion. "Yes, your mom does make the best pumpkin bread in Principio. It's her secret ingredient that makes the bread so moist." Martha, of course, accidentally learned applesauce was Harriet's secret ingredient.

Steven's two children skipped over to their parents to display their very full trick or treat bags. Aaron was costumed as a Tyrannosaurus rex. He bared his tiny teeth and growled every so often. Abby was a doctor in blue scrubs and a white lab coat, with a stethoscope hanging from her neck.

Whatever conversation was about to unfold was halted by the loud explosion of Michael Jackson's *Thriller* filling the night air. The sudden appearance of about 15 teenagers that came out of the darkness and gathered on Main Street drew everyone's attention. In front of the group were festival DJs Ethan and David, their skeleton costumes now glowed in the dark.

Steven asked, "What's happening?" "I don't know," said Jacob as he looked toward Martha, who linked arms with him. "Anyone see Patsy?"

"I did," answered Steven, eyes focused on the assembled group. "Chatted with her briefly as she was backing out of her driveway, responding to an accident on Route 40. She said the twins were fighting colds and would be staying home with Clint. I promised her we'd drop some goody bags off for the children."

"C'mon guys," said Carol, seeing suspicion in the eyes of both men. "They're teenagers. I don't think anything nefarious is going on."

"They're dressed like zombies and with those painted pale green faces they certainly could pass as zombies," observed Martha, and minutes later the reason why became clear.

With Ethan and David in front, the zombies began dancing in unison to the beat of Jackson's famous song. "They're performing a choreographed dance," declared Martha.

Carol giggled and said, "Martha's right."

Bodies swaying, the zombies tilted and snapped their heads, executed a synchronized slide, and then clapped their hands above their heads. They all shifted left, bent their knees, and flung one arm behind and the other in front as they marched forward. More shoulder movements and more forward shuffles followed. Finally, hips were thrust forward, feet were stamped, and arms were outstretched and hands poised as zombie claws.

When it was over, there was thunderous applause. Kids raced toward the zombies, jumping up and down, and tried to imitate the moves they had just watched.

Martha nudged Jacob and asked, "What do you think?"

He smiled down at her, "I think it was the perfect ending to the Principio Furnace Hallowe'en Festival."

Martha left when Carol did with the children. They stopped by Patsy's house and handed Clint two trick or treat bags for the children and bags of cookies, cupcakes, and slices of pumpkin bread for him and Patsy.

Steven and Jacob remained in the square and spent the next hour helping others to clean up the square. All remaining goodies were wrapped up and handed out. Tablecloths were folded and fake candles claimed by their owners. All glass containers were emptied of apple cider and returned to the name of the person written on masking tape on the bottom of the dispenser. The sugar pumpkins that had adorned the tables disappeared quickly. They would end up as pumpkin pie and other desserts.

Tables were broken down and restacked in the bed of the old blue truck. The last table to be broken down was the one where Ethan's computer and portable speakers were set up. Steven and Jacob hung back because Mrs. Rittenhouse was talking to her grandson. Everyone hoped she was praising and not scolding him and his friends for their dance. His friend, David, stood motionless beside him. When she walked away, Jacob and Steven stepped in.

"All okay, Ethan?" asked Jacob.

"Yeah," he answered. "Granny doesn't like surprises."

"Don't we know!" exclaimed Steven. "Jacob and I once put a garter snake in her desk drawer."

"For real?" asked Ethan breaking into a grin.

"For real," acknowledged Steven, as he and Jacob lifted opposite ends of the table and to loaded it into the truck. "Our folks grounded us for a month."

"For two seven-year-olds, it was a brutal punishment," said Jacob.

He and Steven said goodnight and walked away. Jacob barely took seven steps, pivoted, and called back, "You and David did a great job," and then he continued to head home.

2
Storm Warning

Days later, Jacob couldn't name just one thing that had awakened him. Because it was a soft night, he and Martha had cracked open the bedroom window when they retired. He recalled hearing Jackson, Earl and Harriet Johnson's nine-year-old terrier mix, barking incessantly and the wind whistling through the open window.

He didn't recall how long the barking and the whistling went on. Long enough that he finally crawled out of bed, pulled up the blinds, and saw the gentle swaying limbs of the old red maple tree in the back yard and heard the loud rustling of its leaves. And suddenly he knew what was about to happen and he threw himself into action.

He pulled on the black jeans he had flung over the back of the rocking chair the night before. As he wrenched a shirt from the closet, sending the hanger clattering to the floor, he called out to Martha.

"Martha, get up. C'mon, honey, get up and get dressed."

She moaned and turned her head into the pillow. "What time is it?"

"Around 7 a.m.," he told her, tamping down his desire to scream. "Martha, move now."

The tone of Jacob's voice annoyed Martha. Irritated, she dragged herself up to rest on her forearms, surprised to see him dressed. Their two cats, Willy and Dusty, sleeping on a blanket flung across the bottom of the bed, seemed unperturbed by the early morning disruption. Their demeanor changed when Jacob grabbed the four corners of the blanket and bundled them together, ignoring their cries of displeasure.

Jacob tuned out Martha yelling, "Jacob, what are you doing? Jacob!"

He asked her again to hurry and get dressed, adding, "Grab your cell phone, pillows, blankets, and head to the basement."

Without further explanation, he ran down the stairs, moved through the kitchen, and flung open the door to the basement.

Holding the railing with one hand, Jacob descended the steep stairs carrying the blanket holding his feline captives. He deposited the cats in a large old dog kennel in a corner of the basement and locked the kennel door. For added protection, he dragged the kennel closest to the wall behind the stairs, farther away from basement windows.

He hurried back up the stairs only to find Martha blocking the doorway, arms crossed in her classic "don't mess with me" pose. Pillows and blankets were on the floor behind her.

"Martha," Jacob said with strained patience, "I have to go get Harriet, Earl, and Jackson. I need you to call Patsy. Tell her to move Clint and the kids to the basement." Without warning, he grabbed Martha by her upper arms, immobilizing her and promising himself to ask for her forgiveness later. He pivoted, lifted her into the air, and sat his startled wife down near the kitchen sink. "Tell Patsy a storm is coming and to send out a 911."

"What?" demanded Martha in disbelief, "A storm? How do you know a storm is coming?"

"I just do," he answered, kissed her, and without another word dashed out the door, running to the Johnson house.

Martha heard the wind rustling through the leaves of the big red maple and other trees in the woods at the edge of the property. She clutched the front of the full zip sweatshirt she had thrown on as if it was a security blanket. She took a deep breath, unlocked her cell phone, and called Patsy.

Minutes later Jacob was pounding his fist on the Johnson's front door, yelling out their names.

Jackson was still barking.

"Harriet. Earl. Wake up!" Jacob could hear their rapid descent down the wide staircase that was opposite the front door.

Earl, wearing red plaid pajamas, slowly and cautiously opened the door. He was shielding Harriet who stood behind him wearing a matching pair of pajamas. Jackson was panting and pacing back and forth in front of them.

"There's a storm coming," Jacob announced. "I want to get all three of you into our basement." He pushed the door open farther, beckoning the neighbors he'd known for 31 years to follow him.

Husband and wife exchanged a quick look. Wordlessly, Earl bent down, picked up Jackson, reached for Harriet's hand, and fell in step behind Jacob. All three could feel the wind building as Jacob, pulse racing, hurriedly shepherded them toward his house.

Martha, who had been watching from the picture window in the living room, raced to open the front door. She embraced Harriet and ushered her to the basement stairs, going before her in case the older woman fell. Jacob tucked Jackson into the crook of his arm, and offered a hand to help Earl descend the steep stairs. Not surprisingly, Earl rejected the offer.

Jacob directed everyone to huddle in the corner near the dog kennel and ran back upstairs. He stood in the kitchen, pulled out his cell phone, and called

Steven. When there was no answer, he left a message. "Steven. There's a storm coming. I've got your folks and Jackson. We're going to shelter in my basement," and then he disconnected.

The strength of the storm was gathering. It was getting louder. He was about to join everyone in the basement when he remembered 80-year-old Victor Browne, known to most as "Uncle Vic," who lived alone in a one-bedroom apartment behind Babe's Market. The former conductor of the old Philadelphia, Wilmington, and Baltimore Railroad was mostly deaf and used a walker.

Jacob moved halfway down the stairs, stooped slightly, and looked at Martha, Harriet, and Earl. "I've got to see Patsy about Uncle Vic. Don't come upstairs. I'll be back," and he left.

As he ran to Patsy's, bent against the wind, a 911 alert popped up on the screen of his mobile phone. The message was simple. Everyone in their zip code was advised to immediately shelter in place in a basement or a root cellar. Almost simultaneously, he heard the long loud blast of the town's outdoor warning siren. The ear piercing high-tone sound of the siren in itself was alarming. It was signaling danger and could not be ignored. He lifted his eyes skyward, offering a thank you for both his wife for delivering the message to Patsy and for his friend for executing the 911.

Patsy was rolling her police cruiser into her driveway as Jacob ran up. He slapped the palms of his hands on her window. Startled, she looked out at him, and struggled to open the door. The force of the wind was a fierce opponent. Jacob grabbed the door handle and pulled as Patsy pushed.

He said, "Uncle Vic," as she tried to step out. In response, Patsy jerked her head left. Jacob's head snapped right and he felt relief and gratitude seeing the octogenarian sitting in the back seat, a well-worn crocheted granny square afghan draped across his legs.

"I called Babe to let him know I was taking Vic to my house," Patsy said, raising her voice to be heard above the wind. "Can you carry him?"

"Yes," answered Jacob, opening the back door after Patsy unlocked it. "And the walker?"

"Leave it," she answered.

"Grab the door."

She did, and Jacob bent down and gently slid one arm behind Uncle Vic's back and under his arms, and the other under his legs. He carefully lifted him and removed him from the back seat. Jacob was too aware of the fragility of the old man who time had not been kind to. He was pale, his cheeks sunken, and his eyes no longer sparkled.

As the throw started to slip to the ground, Uncle Vic moaned. He muttered something in a dry raspy voice and reached out a thin bony hand to catch the falling throw. Patsy swooped in, snatched it up, and then stepped back to give Jacob and his delicate cargo a clear path to her front door.

The wind, which had grown in strength, hampered Jacob's journey. Every few steps he stumbled slightly but quickly recovered and moved forward. Patsy opened the heavy oak door, only to have it torn from her hands by a sudden gust of wind. She tried to open it again, yelling at the top of her lungs for Clint to come help her.

Jacob never understood how Clint heard Patsy, but he did. Even above the wind, Clint could be heard shouting for Patsy as he charged up the stairs from the basement. Together, they were able to brace the door open and give Jacob time to slip in and to carry Uncle Vic into the house and down to the basement.

Jacob carefully deposited Uncle Vic in an old recliner. Nearby, the children were sleeping and huddled together atop some pillows and under several layers of blankets on an old loveseat. Clint bent down and stroked the heads of his children, assuring himself they were safe for the time being.

"I've got to go home," Jacob said, still hearing the blaring siren and watching Patsy drape the treasured throw over Uncle Vic's lap and legs. She placed a blanket on top of the throw and gently took one of Uncle Vic's hands in hers.

She glanced at Vic with undisguised sadness and then made direct eye contact with Jacob. He read the unspoken message in her eyes and felt his heart sink. "Go," she said and he did.

Although the distance between Patsy's house and Jacob's was barely six feet, Jacob felt as if he was at the beach slugging through wet sand as he tried to get home. Walking upright was nearly impossible.

He reached the steps to his porch, gripped the railing with both hands, and as if playing a game of tug of war, used a hand over hand action to pull and fight his way to the top. Crossing the porch to the front door proved to be just as difficult.

Jacob fought to reach the door. He repeatedly threw his body forward, arms outstretched, trying to grasp the brass door handle. When he finally connected with it with his left hand, he used his right hand to turn the doorknob. Nothing happened. Exhausted, he sent out a prayer for help and it was in that very moment he realized the storm had landed.

The next time he twisted the knob, the door opened just enough for him to see Earl standing on the other side. The older man was using the full weight of his body to pull open the door. With Jacob pushing and Earl pulling, the door opened wide enough for Jacob to squeeze through.

The door slammed shut with a loud bang, rattling windows. "Thank you," said Jacob as he paused to catch his breath. Earl was still leaning against the door, bent over and clutching his knees for support.

"Don't know how you knew I needed help, but I'm glad you did."

"Martha," said Earl. "She heard the door slamming."

Jacob looked at him and said, "Let's get downstairs."

When they reached the bottom of the basement stairs, Jacob saw the terror on the faces of the two women. They sat shoulder to shoulder on a thick memory foam pad, usually stored in a spare bedroom upstairs. There was a stack of blankets nearby. Jacob also saw a bowl of water and food had been put in the kennel for Willy and Dusty. Water and treats also were on the floor for Jackson.

Earl grabbed a blanket and sat beside his wife, pulling her and a trembling Jackson closer. He kissed his wife and gave the top of Jackson's head a soft knuckle rub to calm him.

Harriet looked up at Jacob and asked, "Victor?"

"At Patsy's," he answered.

Jacob dropped down next to Martha and captured her hands in his. He felt her tense as they heard the sharp crack and crash of a tree. And then another and another. Selfishly, he hoped none was the red maple, which his parents had planted to commemorate his birth.

Shaking, Martha snuggled closer and turned her head into the crook of Jacob's neck. They heard glass breaking, shingles being ripped from the roof, and the sound of unknown objects being slammed into the brick walls of the house. In the distance they could hear rumbling like rolling thunder and a roar that mimicked the sound of a jet. There were more violent crashes, and they could only guess at the source. Seven minutes later there was dead silence.

No one moved. Jacob and Earl exchanged looks.

"I need to check on Patsy and her family," Jacob announced.

Earl stood. "I'll go with you."

Jacob, knowing Earl would not take no for an answer, looked at Harriet and Martha, saying, "Stay here."

When they stepped outside, they were shocked. Wind, fierce and relentless, had torn through Principio Furnace, tearing through wooden structures like a row of stacked dominoes, pitching anything not locked down into the air. Trees had been uprooted. Power lines were toppled, blocking streets. Debris littered the streets and sidewalks.

"This wasn't a windstorm," said Jacob.

"No," agreed Earl. "It wasn't."

Jacob was about to step forward when he saw Patsy walking toward him.

She held up her hand, saying, "We're okay. I've called the Barracks. Ambulances and emergency responders have been dispatched. The first ambulance will be coming to my house."

In the distance, they heard the uninterrupted wailing of sirens from police cars and ambulances.

"Your house?" said Earl, registering alarm, but Jacob understood.

"Uncle Vic," he said and clamped a hand over his mouth, holding back his emotions. He sighed and dropped his head to his chest. Watching Jacob's reaction to Patsy's news, Earl reached out and placed a reassuring hand on his shoulder.

"Yes," Patsy said sadly. "He closed his eyes and died, one hand clutching that afghan."

Curious, Earl asked, "An old afghan? Different colors of yarn and made of granny squares?"

"Yes," said Patsy, surprised. "You know it?"

"Yes, I do. His wife, Ann, made it," explained Earl, "for their son, Clay. But Clay died in Vietnam. Victor once told me when Ann passed that afghan was the only possession he had that still connected him to his wife and son. I'm so happy you were with him at the end, Patsy."

Jacob was about to add "Me, too" when he heard a car door slam behind him. He turned to see Steven jogging toward them, calling out, "Dad."

Earl broke away from Patsy, stepped in front of Jacob, and extended his arms to embrace his son. After a hearty hug, Steven pulled back and asked,

"Where's Mom?"

No one answered him. Everyone's attention was fixed on the site of an ambulance, lights flashing, siren blaring, tearing down the road behind Steven.

3

Inherited Ability Revealed

IN THE BASEMENT, MARTHA FOUGHT BACK a desire to race after Jacob, feeling obligated to remain with Harriet. She could see the strain on the face of the woman, who even in her 60s, still showed her beauty.

"Mrs. Johnson," started Martha, only to be interrupted.

"Harriet, Martha. Just Harriet."

Martha flashed a smile and corrected herself. "Harriet." She paused and added, "I'm curious. Why did you and Mr. Johns . . . Earl immediately respond when Jacob came to your door telling you a storm was coming?"

"Experience," she answered, grabbing a treat off the floor for Jackson.

"Experience?" It wasn't what Martha expected to hear. "And Patsy, who didn't hesitate to take my call and said, 'Done' when I passed along Jacob's message? Would she also claim it was experience?"

"Yes, dear. Experience and history." Harriet pulled the blanket more tightly around herself.

Martha scooted over to the edge of the mattress and picked up another blanket. She draped it over Harriet's shoulders.

"You must be cold in those pajamas." They were a light-weight cotton, not a cozy flannel.

"A bit," replied Harriet, as she reached behind to pull the blanket down her back, and then over her head of short curly brown hair.

"What do mean experience and history?"

"Oh, you know dear," she said, but Martha didn't. "Know what?"

It was Harriet's turn to be surprised by the question. She gazed into Martha's eyes and was reminded of the color of the horse chestnuts she and her grandchildren collected in fall for the squirrels. "Why know that Jacob has the sixth sense."

A confused Martha, eyebrows raised, said, "The sixth sense? There are only five senses." Finger by finger she counted them out. "Sight, sound, smell, taste, and hearing."

"And the powerful sixth sense," stated Harriet matter-of-factly. "Some people call it perception, others intuition. Jacob's mother, Eve, had it."

Harriet's closing words jarred Martha. She had briefly met the parents of the man she married 18 months before. The information was totally new to her and rather unsettling. Harriet was exposing a facet of Jacob's character she knew nothing about.

Trying to wrap her brain around Harriet's statements, Martha was about to ask Harriet to provide details when she heard the wail of an ambulance siren. It was close. Too close.

Hearing it too, Harriet sat Jackson down on the floor. Both the women immediately stood. Harriet threw her hands over her heart.

Martha reached out, took Harriet's left hand, said, "Come on," and led her up the stairs. They walked into the living room, stopping in front of the picture window framed on both sides by narrow, antique leaded glass panels. Jackson charged up the stairs behind them, coming to rest at Harriet's feet.

Both women were relieved to see their husbands on the sidewalk talking with Patsy. Harriet cried out, "Oh, my," seeing her son, Steven, fast stepping to reach his father. Even Martha felt a rush of emotion when she watched Earl turn away from Patsy, step in front of Jacob, and extend his arms to embrace his son.

Neither Martha nor Harriet could hear what Steven said to his father but saw both men shift their attention to the two women standing at the window in the Biddle house. Jacob and Patsy also turned.

Harriet actually sprinted, beating Martha, Earl, Steven, and Jacob to the front door. The Johnson family had a group hug on the porch with Jackson barking and begging to be included in the reunion.

Jacob came up the stairs and hugged Martha as if he hadn't seen her in months. It had barely been fifteen minutes.

"The ambulance?" asked Martha, praying that Clint, the children, and the man they called Uncle Vic were okay.

"For Victor," said Jacob, and heard Harriet let out a sob.

Earl explained, "Patsy said he went in his sleep."

"So a gentle passage," remarked Harriet. She bent her head, closed her eyes, and said a simple prayer, asking for the Heavenly Father to accept Victor Browne into his kingdom and grant him eternal peace.

Everyone said Amen.

Jacob was the first to break the silence. "I'd like to go back and help Patsy. She got the ambulance here to take Uncle Vic to Crouch's in North East. But there's so much damage and we need to see if people need help."

Earl and Steven said they were both ready to help.

"So am I," said Martha, arms crossed.

"And me," said Harriet, lifting her chin.

All three men looked uncomfortable, all reluctant to respond.

"Mom, don't you think you and Dad need to

change?" suggested Steven, successfully cutting through the awkwardness of the moment.

"Of course," agreed Harriet, directing Steven to pick up Jackson. "We'll all meet up here after Dad and I change."

No one objected. It would be foolish if they did.

Martha turned to Jacob, "I'll go over to Patsy's with you until the Johnsons return. I'm sorry about Uncle Vic."

Jacob said, "My parents often had the Browne family to dinner. After Uncle Vic lost his son and his wife, he joined us after church every Sunday for dinner."

When they saw two men exit Patsy's house with the wheeled stretcher and a body bag on top, they joined Patsy on the sidewalk.

Martha reached out to Patsy, knowing Jacob considered her to be the sister he never had. "The children?"

"Safe. Clint took them upstairs to dress. They don't understand what's going on. And other than telling them there was a really bad storm, I don't think any other explanation is necessary."

Jacob and Martha didn't have long to wait for the return of the Johnsons. Gone were the matching pajamas. In their place were jeans, shirts, and jackets. Slippers were replaced with sturdy boots.

Harriet came to stand beside Martha. She frowned, saying, "Not one piece of my fall decorations survived!"

"Nor mine," said Martha in sympathy. She had been quite fond of the old weathered wooden bucket that held the huge planter of white chrysanthemums. Foolishly, she had hoped it had survived.

Martha chastised herself for even having such a frivolous thought. She looked back to see Jacob standing behind the ambulance, his arms wrapped around Patsy in a gesture of comfort. Both stood silently, watching the white ambulance with the bold red stripe along its side that looked like an oversized van travel down the road, emergency lights flashing, until it was out of sight. The Johnson family also watched the departure.

Patsy reached out and patted Jacob's right hand that rested on her upper arm. "I'm going to check on my children, my husband," she said, "And after that, I'll start moving toward the heart of town and assess the damage."

"Before you do," Jacob said, "can you confirm that someone called PIW Utilities to cut off power to Principio? Any one of those downed lines could still be live."

"I'll call the Barracks and confirm that has been done. No one," Patsy warned, making direct eye contact with each person, "is to move forward until I have an answer to that question."

When Patsy went into her house, Jacob said, "Let's assess the damage to our properties."

Everyone moved to the Johnson house, encircling it like a group of insurance inspectors. The sheer number of shingles on the ground was daunting. As if they were connected by some invisible wire, their heads moved in unison as they looked up at the roof and saw the patches of missing asphalt shingles. They also saw there was substantial damage to the chimney.

"Lucky," said Earl as he bent and picked up some shingles, "that we didn't lose the roof."

"Very lucky," Steven added, picking up more shingles and throwing them in a pile toward the center of the property.

As their property inspection continued, no one saw a broken window or a broken door. What they did see was the tool shed in the backyard completely demolished, crushed by several large limbs ripped from the trunk of the oak tree. A rope swing with a rusted red metal seat still hung from one of its limbs.

Upon seeing the downed swing, Harriet frowned and said, "This won't make the grandchildren happy."

"It doesn't make me happy, Mom," protested Steven. "I shared that swing with my brothers and Jacob and Patsy."

The wooden fencing that had separated the Johnson and Biddle properties for decades became the next center of attention. It no longer was upright but lay in broken sections across the two yards.

There were more shingles on the ground in Jacob's yard and his concern about what they would find in the heart of Principio Furnace grew. He was grateful to find the red maple undamaged and silently offered a prayer of thanks. At the back of the property multiple birch trees were felled.

Banged up galvanized metal garbage cans that no one recognized were in the yard. Broken terra-cotta planters, splintered bird houses, and pieces of pumpkin were everywhere. And firewood Jacob had neatly stacked in crisscross fashion months before was strewn across his, the Johnson's and the Greyson's yards.

Similar items were found in the Greyson back yard, including lots of shingles. A new Radio Flyer red wagon, a birthday gift to Charlotte and William from Martha and Jacob, lay nearby twisted and upside down. Several wheels were bent. And a glance at Clint's tabletop grill showed it would have to be replaced.

It wasn't Patsy Greyson, wife, mother, and child-hood friend who stepped out her back door and looked at the damage with them. Instead, it was Captain Patricia Armour. She wore a long-sleeve, tan-colored shirt with a black tie tucked into belted olive pants with a black stripe down the side. Her dark brown hair was in a neat French twist under a felt Stetson hat.

"It could have been so much worse," she said. No one disagreed with her. "For safety, the power grid for Principio Furnace has been shut down. PIW Utilities is sending out resources to efficiently restore power, so we can all walk into the heart of town and . . ."

Martha interrupted her without apology. "Before we go anywhere, there's something we need to talk about."

Patsy displayed a flash of temper. She wanted to get to town and assist her fellow officers and other emergency responders, not have some conversation with Martha. "What do we need to talk about?"

"Jacob."

"Me?" said Jacob, genuinely shocked.

"You," answered Martha. "Let's step inside our house for a quick discussion." Without another word, she walked past Jacob and the Johnsons and opened the front door. They all followed, with Patsy bringing up the rear.

In the house, they gathered in the dining room. Only Harriet and Earl took a seat at the table.

"Martha," Jacob, who stood apart from his wife, started and she quickly cut him off.

"No, Jacob," she said, "Don't interrupt me." Her hostile tone and stern words shocked everyone, but no one more than her husband.

"By this evening, Principio Furnace will be the next headline in local papers certainly, and in national publications most likely. News crews are probably already mobilized, ready to move into town like bloodhounds tracking the scent of a story, except there's no missing child, no escaped prisoner. What there is the aftermath of a violent destructive storm. A freak storm."

Martha settled her gaze on Patsy, who stood, legs slightly apart, with her hands clasped in front of her. "And how do you explain, Patsy, in the absence of any real scientific evidence, that a 911 alert was released and the local warning siren activated a good—what, eight to ten minutes—before the storm landed? "

All were dumbfounded, but she didn't stop there. "No one," declared Martha, and she watched Harriet's face drain of color, "can reveal my husband as the source of your information. So we must all agree, here and now, on a plausible explanation."

"Martha," said Jacob, shaking his head, attempting appeasement, "what are you doing?"

"Protecting our privacy and preventing anyone in this room from stating that you, Jacob, had a *feeling* that a storm was coming and requested an alert be sent out to warn people," she snapped, pointing a finger at him.

When no one spoke, she continued. "So here and now we shore up a story and ensure there are no leaks. You, Jacob, are not going to be breaking news at 5 p.m. on Channel 13."

There was a long silence and then Patsy said, "Martha is right," and sighed heavily. "The timing raises questions. Does anyone have any ideas?"

With Patsy's words, there was no satisfaction in Martha's face, no softening in her demeanor. Her heart-shaped face showed determination; her mouth remained set in a firm line.

Jacob, hands gripping the top of a dining room chair, spoke, directing his question to everyone but Martha. "Remember when I spent the summer in Dutch Harbor working as a member of the yard crew for a company that served the fishing vessels when I was in my 20s?"

Having grown up in Washington State, Martha knew exactly where Dutch Harbor was, and what it was.

"I do," said Steven, and then said accusingly, "I wanted to join you, but Mom objected."

"Yes," answered Harriet defensively. "Both your father and I felt it was too far for you to go for summer employment."

"People in Dutch describe it as the place where the wind is born," Jacob continued. "After an event that happened in July that year, I believe it. And I think that experience could justify the call to Patsy."

"Let's hear it," Patsy told him.

"It was a beautiful day. Blue sky, calm water in the bay. There were no boats at dock. I was going to town to pick up the mail and some supplies with the office manager, Renee. She had her two dogs with her and when we pulled away from the office, both started barking furiously. I had a tremendous headache. Later I learned that some people get a raging headache when there's a drop in barometric pressure. I qualify as one of those people."

Jacob paused before continuing. "Renee had just turned left off Captains Bay Road and was crossing the bridge to the other side, when out of nowhere a windstorm hit. A storm with winds clocked at 120 miles per hour that barely lasted fifteen minutes. It was bizarre. I watched the roof of an industrial building a good mile beyond where we were be lifted in the air and deposited in the road in front of us. Fortunately, we were caught between two small hills that protected us."

"I was reminded of that experience last night. It was the combination of Jackson barking, having a really nasty headache, the wind whistling through the window, and the rumbling of thunder in the distance, that prompted my request for a 911 alert."

"So now we have a story," said Martha.

"Yes," Patsy acknowledged, "we do. And this is how I'll spin it." Patsy laid it out and everyone agreed to the script.

"I don't know about anyone else," said Earl as he pushed away from the table and stood, "but I'm ready to walk to town and see what help is needed."

Harriet and Steven joined Earl and so did Patsy. They looked at Martha, waiting for her to move forward.

"I need to free the fur babies from the kennel downstairs, so I'll catch up. Go with them, Jacob."

"I'll wait for you, Martha." And he did.

4

Assessing Storm Damage

IT DIDN'T TAKE HOURS FOR NEWS about the pre-dawn storm that hit Principio Furnace to flood the airwaves. Jacob had been right. It wasn't a windstorm. According to the National Weather Service it was an EF2 tornado with winds exceeding 110 miles per hour. In the end, only 20 houses were completely demolished, although none escaped some degree of damage. Fortunately, there were no fatalities or injuries directly tied to the tornado.

Newer houses in the community, many built fifteen years to twenty years ago but not made of brick and mortar, took the biggest punch. Wood siding had been peeled back from their frames like adhesive labels on a package. Whole walls were missing, roofs ripped off, stone chimneys reduced to piles of rubble, interior structures gutted, and their contents tossed out like celebratory confetti. Yards and streets were littered with remnants of people's lives—treasures and memories.

While a team of emergency responders who were part of a multi-county strike team performed a house-by-house search checking on occupants and assessing damage, a reporter with a microphone and a cameraman were right on their heels. It didn't take hours for Martha's prediction of reporters digging for an explanation about the 911 alert and the warning siren to be realized. Nearly every adult interviewed credited the survival of their families, pets included, to receiving that early morning alert. It took little time for reporters to discover that the National Weather Service had not predicted any storm for the area other than the possibility of rain and maybe a thunderstorm the next evening. And it took even less time for them to find the link to Captain Patricia Armour.

Someone in the throng of reporters who had descended on Principio was overheard remarking that reporters were the human equivalent of bloodhounds. They were so correct. Reporters representing local papers like the Cecil Courier, regional papers like the Baltimore Star, and even The Washington Post who wrote articles for print and online versions of their publications were present. Each carried a byline story about the freak tornado that had ravaged the bedroom community of Principio Furnace.

The story narrative was relatively consistent. It described people, some with pets, who sheltered in root cellars and basements and heard what sounded like a freight train barreling through the community that had no train tracks. When the noise stopped, people crawled out of their temporary shelters, some on their hands and knees, some bent, but upright. Some crawled out cradling children, animals, and each other. All surveyed the damage and were shaken by the devastation they saw. So were Jacob and Martha who stood, transfixed, hands tightly entwined to form a fisted knot of solidarity. It was one thing to view the aftermath of a natural disaster on TV, and another to see it firsthand and to smell the fear.

Jacob and Martha checked on two Biddle farm employees, Miller Newton and Isaiah Titter, and their families. Thankfully, the homes of both had sustained little damage. Caitlyn, another employee, was with her father, the town's mayor, David Spence, in Philadelphia on family business. David had already called one of the town's two commissioners to say the family was on the road and heading home.

As they continued to check on members of the community, Martha picked up pictures and other personal items from the ground and placed them in a canvas tote Jacob was carrying in hopes they could be reunited with their owners. There were so many people milling about Martha and Jacob felt they were adding to the chaos of the situation despite a highly organized response. They expressed that opinion to Steven when they ran into him traversing the town square where just the night before they had gathered to celebrate Hallowe'en.

"Did you hear that it was a tornado?" asked Steven with undisguised incredulity as his eyes moved across the shredded landscape.

"Insane," answered Jacob, punctuating his response by throwing his hands in the air.

"A weather aberration," Martha added. "Some reporter said it was a meteorological phenomenon, whatever that means." She thought she'd do an Internet search of the term later.

Steven said he agreed with both of them.

"Have you eaten anything," Martha asked, "because I can offer you a banana, an energy bar, or both?"

"Really?" said Steven and when she nodded yes, he said, "I wouldn't mind an energy bar."

Martha brushed aside the thick single braid the color of burnished copper that hung over her right shoulder to access a black nylon backpack. She unzipped the bag and took out a bar for Steven and one for Jacob as well.

"Where are your parents?" asked Jacob.

"Home, I hope," said Steven. "Both were very stressed after seeing the damage, especially Mom."

"It's pretty upsetting," commented Martha.

"When Mom saw Babe's Market and the apartment Uncle Vic lived in, she cried."

"We saw the store's picture window was shattered, but didn't walk around back to see what happened to his apartment," said Jacob.

"There is no apartment," responded Steven. "It was completely demolished. Flattened like a pancake. He would have been killed. Crushed to death or worse."

"Oh, no," choked out Martha.

"I am grateful Patsy got him before the storm . . . tornado . . . hit," Jacob said, "and that he died peacefully with her holding his hand."

"I'm not sure Mom knew about Patsy holding his hand. Mom was more exhausted than I've ever seen her. Dad insisted they go home so she could rest."

"And you?" asked Martha.

"Carol's been calling," he told her, unwrapping the energy bar. "I assured her we're all safe, but she wants me home."

"There's not much we can do here other than offer hope and sympathy. I saw Pastor Drew consoling people, and the mayor of Perryville directing people to shelters in the area," Martha added as she moved in the direction of home.

Jacob and Steven flanked her like human bookends, leading her around fallen trees, at times helping her climb over them. As they approached a downed power line, all were more cautious. The men speculated on how long it could be before needed repairs were made and the time they suggested made Martha say, "So we have to be prepared to be without power for a day or more?" Simultaneously, both said, "Yes."

Jacob added, "It's a possibility."

"I need to check on Mom and Dad before I leave the area," said Steven. "They and Jackson can stay with us."

"Betcha they reject that idea," smiled Jacob.

Steven smiled and nodded in agreement. "Betcha you're right. But I'll still ask. What about you two?"

"We'll be fine won't we, Martha?"

"Yes," Martha said, looking skyward and seeing blue skies and no clouds.

"Although it appears the central area of Principio took the brunt of the tornado, we need to check the farm for damage and to make sure the backup generator is working," Jacob said.

"If we're going to be without electricity, we can pick up some food in Perryville," suggested Martha. "When we reach town, we can check to see if Harriet and Earl want anything."

"Sounds good," said Steven, as he turned to walk up to his childhood home. "I'll definitely be back tomorrow to start clean up."

Martha and Jacob gave a quick wave good-bye and then went into their house. They quickly checked on Willy and Dusty and then collected their phone chargers. Before leaving, they gathered all their flashlights and placed them on the dining table along with some camping lanterns Jacob retrieved from the basement. He also made sure there were logs, kindling, and a lighter staged near the fireplace.

Less than ten minutes later they were in the SUV and driving west on Route 7 to the farm. Surprisingly, there were no trees blocking the roads, no downed power lines. When they pulled into the parking lot of the farm twenty minutes later, everything appeared intact, just as it had when they left the evening before. The fruit and vegetable stand with its huge overhead garage doors at the front was still secure.

Jacob drove behind the concrete block structure, parking near the single door at the back. Both he and Martha got out of the car. Jacob moved to the industrial steel door and unlocked the first of two deadbolts. As he did, Martha called out that she was going to check out the pumpkin patch, which was to the left of the stand and behind several commercial trucks used to distribute pumpkins.

He had just stepped inside and flipped on the two light switches when Martha screamed out his name. For an instant Jacob's heart stopped. He spun on his heels and ran out the door, his blood pumping, and headed in the direction of the pumpkin patch. He saw Martha dashing toward what looked like an old black stovepipe sticking out of the ground at the center of the patch. He followed her and as he closed the distance between them, he immediately understood why she screamed.

Sitting atop a mound of peat moss that had been dumped after they had planted flower starters was a barefoot toddler wearing only shorts and a blue T-shirt with a smiling, lime colored dinosaur plastered across the front. The child, with a helmet of coal black curly hair that looked like corkscrews, was sobbing and gnawing on his left hand.

"Jacob," Martha called out calmly as she slowly stepped toward the child, "grab a blanket from the back seat."

Moments later Jacob returned, unfolded a medium-weight plaid blanket and told Martha to pick up the child. She was surprised to find the child was heavier than she expected. Jacob wrapped the blanket around the child and then took possession of him.

"He's cold, Jacob," Martha said as she unfolded the second blanket and covered the child with it for a second layer of protection.

Jacob moved to the back seat of the SUV and Martha, interpreting his intent, opened the door and crawled in. When she was seated, he placed the child on her lap, and pulled out the seat belt as far as possible until he could secure the lock.

"Comfortable?" Jacob asked and she nodded yes as she cradled the child's head and gently pressed him against her chest. His choking sobs now were stuttered cries interspersed with tiny gulps.

"We need to alert the police, Martha."

Ignoring Jacob's statement, Martha said, "We need to take him to Dr. Howards in Perryville."

Jacob took a deep breath, closed the passenger door, locked the back door to the stand, and then got in the driver's seat.

"Jacob," Martha said as he turned over the engine, "Please call Dr. Howard's private number and tell her we're on the way to her office with an abandoned toddler." And before he pulled out onto West bound Route 7, he did just that, only to learn she wasn't at the clinic, but seeing patients at the hospital for the day.

Despite the urgency of the situation, Jacob maintained the speed limit, so it took more than thirty minutes to drive the 25 miles to the hospital on the outskirts of Perryville. His gaze shifted between the road ahead and the rear-view mirror. Every so often Martha's chestnut brown eyes locked with his bluish gray eyes. Her face registered concern as evidenced by her furrowed brows and the hard, straight line of her lips.

The child's sobs had stopped and Jacob thought it

was because he was nestled comfortably at Martha's bosom. The blankets no longer covered his head and all that was visible was an explosion of black curls. Jacob could see the child had latched onto Martha's single braid as if it were a lifeline, and perhaps, thought Jacob, it was just that. He had no doubt Martha would defend the child's life if it was threatened while he was in her care.

There were three other cars in the parking lot of the TriCity Hospital and Medical Clinic when Jacob rolled in. It was Dr. Jill, the tall, black, and stunningly beautiful daughter of Old Doc Johnson, who stood in the reception area to greet Jacob and Martha and their special package. Wearing a white coat and a stethoscope around her neck, she stopped to take a folder from the woman behind the counter, who along with the two occupants in the area, stared at Jacob and Martha with curiosity. In a corner there was a television airing a news broadcast of the events in Principio Furnace.

"Martha, Jacob," said Dr. Howard, as she directed them to follow her through a door and into a hallway with exam rooms on both sides. "We've been watching the news being broadcast about the disaster in Principio Furnace all day. Even caught a glimpse of both of you walking in front of Babe's Market. Unbelievable damage."

When she opened the door to the second exam

room on the right, Martha and Jacob stepped in. The doctor directed Martha to place the child on a flat exam table in the center of the room. Blankets and all, Martha set the child down, but didn't release her hold.

"We had no idea we had been caught on camera," Jacob said in surprise as he watched Dr. Howard pull on exam gloves she removed from a box stacked in a rack near a counter.

"I called Chief Cox," said Dr. Howard, and when she heard Martha say "Doctor," she held up her hand to pause any objection, "because by law I'm required to do so. Everyone is in Principio," she continued, "but an officer will be dispatched here as soon as possible. A report must be filed and an investigation initiated."

"Martha," said Dr. Howard firmly and she threw a look at Jacob that clearly said, "help me." "I need to examine the child, so you need to let go."

Jacob moved behind Martha and placed his hands on her shoulders, gently pulling her back toward him. Dr. Howard gently removed the child's hand that gripped Martha's braid.

"Where did you find him?" asked the doctor as she removed the child's shirt, examining his back and torso.

Jacob answered, "Martha found him in the middle of our pumpkin patch."

Dr. Howard's head snapped up, "In the pumpkin

patch?"

"Near a broken section of a stovepipe," added Martha who held her hands, interlocked and index fingers forming a steeple, in front of her face.

"My goodness, this child certainly has an abundance of hair! Visually the child looks healthy. No bruises, no cuts. But I need to admit him to the hospital . . ."

Martha cut her off, "The hospital?"

"I don't know if there are internal injuries. The child needs to be fed and bathed and dressed in clean clothes."

"Peat can come home with us," said Martha.

Both Jacob and Dr. Howard said with alarm, "Peat?"

"Yes," Martha answered. "I decided to call him Peat because I found him on that block of peat moss."

Jacob barely had time to flinch. "We can't keep him, Martha. This isn't a stray cat or a stray dog. This is a child."

"I know it's a child. A child who the Good Lord has placed in our care."

Marshalling his patience, he closed his eyes and took a deep breath. "Martha, it's been a long and trying day. I'm thankful we found the child, but there are laws that must be followed."

"I know there are laws. But there is no greater law than loving and caring for children, no matter how they're delivered!"

Not waiting for a response, Martha added, "Admit it. There is something special about this child."

"We don't know that," responded Jacob.

"I do," declared Martha. "Look at the birthmark."

"What birthmark?"

"This one," said Dr. Howard, as she pulled down the child's shorts to reveal his navel.

Jacob moved closer to view the mark.

"It looks like. . ." Jacob paused, as if reluctant to describe what he saw.

Martha on the other hand didn't hesitate. "It looks like a pumpkin tendril!"

"Yes," agreed Dr. Howard, "it looks exactly like a finely etched pumpkin tendril."

And at that moment there was a knock on the door with a nurse announcing the arrival of Perryville's Chief of Police Ken Cox.

5

Abandoned Child

J ACOB STEPPED INTO THE HALLWAY AND shook the hand of Chief Ken Cox and recalled meeting him in early October when he brought his young daughter and wife to the Pumpkin Patch at the Biddle Farm. For many, the man dispelled some misconceptions about the appearance and character of police, especially in rural communities. A slight but physically fit man, the chief was barely 35, a homegrown boy, and a war hero who had a prosthetic left leg and chose the mantle of law enforcement over redeployment.

The chief glanced in the exam room and saw the child, who he estimated to be two to three years old, sitting on the exam table and munching what he recognized as Goldfish cheddar crackers. The most visible feature of the light-skinned child with chubby cheeks was a shocking abundance of curly black hair.

He told the audience of three that before leaving the station he had checked current records and there were no amber alerts issued in Cecil or surrounding counties for a missing child. He then asked Jacob when, where, and at what time the child was found. After Jacob said his wife, Martha, had actually discovered the toddler, Ken looked at the young woman who turned her head and faced him when she heard her name. Seeing her skin tone and hair color, Ken wondered if, like his own wife, Martha Biddle could claim Irish ancestry. Because of the events in Principio Furnace, it wasn't surprising that her attractive face showed signs of severe fatigue and distress. But when their eyes locked momentarily, he hadn't expected to see such undisguised sadness.

He directed a battery of questions to Jacob. *Before this morning, when were you last at the farm? Why did you to go to the property this morning? Did you see any vehicle, any person, when you approached, entered, or left the farm? Did you notice anything, other than the stovepipe, that was out of place?*

The questions ended with Chief Cox recording Jacob's home address and mobile number in his pocket-size notebook, and saying, "For now, I have all the information I need. If you remember anything, please call me." He handed Jacob his business card, adding "I'll go to the farm and look around. I may see something neither of you did."

Turning to face Dr. Howard, he asked if she intended to place the child in the pediatric ward at the hospital. When Dr. Howard answered yes, Martha quickly jumped into the conversation.

"We can wait until you've completed your exam, Dr. Howard, and then take the boy into our care until his family is found."

Shocked, Jacob could only stare at Martha but was saved from contradicting her because Chief Cox said firmly, "That's not possible, Mrs. Biddle. There are procedures . . ."

"We're approved to be foster . . .," she snapped back only to have Jacob cut her off.

"Martha," said Jacob, "Dr. Howard has this under control. So does Chief Cox. We need to pick up some food and go home. We can talk to Dr. Howard tomorrow."

"We can rent a room here tonight, Jacob."

It was Chief Cox's turn to interrupt. "Mrs. Biddle, there are no rooms available in Perryville or in North East. Those that were are now filled with residents of Principio affected by this morning's tornado. Principio still has no power and according to PIW Utilities it could be tomorrow or the next day before power is restored."

The news successfully silenced Martha. Her shoulders drooped and her jaw tightened. She looked defeated.

"I'll update you both later," Dr. Howard said as she watched Jacob plant a kiss on the top of Martha's head, and then wrap his arms around her shoulders and escort her out.

On their exit, Chief Cox closed the door. "I don't want you to violate any privacy laws, but Martha Biddle seemed very intense."

The doctor stood over the child that was now asleep, gently stroking his back, and said, "I'm sure the natural disaster in Principio Furnace today didn't help. But let me give you some history. My father was James and Eve Biddle's family doctor. He delivered Jacob and I babysat him. After his parents died, he returned to Principio Furnace with his wife, Martha, who is from the Pacific Northwest. A little over a year ago, Martha had a miscarriage, and shortly thereafter she and Jacob approached me about becoming foster parents. I, along with Dr. Drew in North East, and Captain Patricia Armour with the Maryland State Police, sponsored them. They fulfilled all the state requirements and are qualified to be foster parents."

"I see," said the chief, rubbing the back of this neck.

"There's more. During the interview process, I learned that Martha had been married before and was a widow. Her husband and 2-year-old child, a boy, died when their vehicle was struck by a drunk driver as they were driving home."

Ken Cox dropped his head, now understanding it wasn't just sadness he saw in Martha Biddle's eyes. It was raw pain, unresolved grief. Truthfully he said, "I can't imagine losing a child and then finding one—a boy no less—abandoned. That had to trigger a whole lot of heartache."

"Exactly."

"Before I take a drive to the Biddle Farm, I need to take his picture, and I'll need DNA."

"Bloodwork is on my check list." As an afterthought, she added, "The child has a rather unique birthmark that I would suggest be kept secret." He agreed when he saw it. "In my opinion, only a parent or a relative would know about it."

After leaving Dr. Howard and the boy at the hospital, Chief Cox checked in with his on-duty officer. He instructed the officer to distribute the picture he was sending him to the media and to simply state that an abandoned child was found in the area. When his officer pressed for more information, the Chief told him just to add the department's phone number, no other details. After telling the officer he'd check in with him later, he headed to the Biddle Farm to begin his investigation.

He had forgotten how large the parking lot was in front of the Biddle Farm produce stand. Thirty cars could easily be accommodated. The farm was so packed in October that he had been forced to park along the road. Many of the decorations set up for Hallowe'en at the farm were still in place. In the back right corner was a wooden scarecrow and pumpkin cutout where he had captured a picture of his wife and daughter. Behind it was a shiny 1950 Black Ford truck with the name Biddle Farms emblazoned in white lettering across the door with a bright graphic of three pumpkins below it.

And when he drove to the back of the building, he was surprised that on his last visit he failed to notice not only a warehouse, but also a good-sized greenhouse. He later would learn, and it surprised him, that Biddle Farms included a produce packing, cold storage, and a distribution facility.

He exited his vehicle, and stood, hands on hips, and surveyed his surroundings as if he was a cartographer mapping the area. Although not officially a crime scene, he treated it as if it was. He approached the large pumpkin patch and used his cell phone to capture the image of the stovepipe next to a block of peat moss. It was just as Jacob Biddle had described it.

Ken crouched and carefully examined the pipe that normally provided a passageway for gases to travel from a connected stove to a chimney. Several aspects about the presence of the stovepipe disturbed him and it gave rise to speculation.

He was committed to finding answers to the avalanche of questions that ran though his brain like a rock tumbler.

It took considerable time to search the pumpkin patch, but other than the stovepipe, he found nothing out of place, not even a discarded candy wrapper. He spent the next hour carefully walking the perimeter of the patch, which included searching a very old grove of sycamore trees.

With careful deliberation he moved slowly and explored the grove of trees and stopped when he found what he had suspected would be there all along. After snapping a few more pictures, he went back to the pumpkin patch. He pulled on disposable gloves and placed the stovepipe in the large plastic bag he had tucked into his back pocket. The stovepipe would be submitted as scientific evidence with the hope, however remote, that some fingerprints could be found and that running the prints through the national Automated Fingerprint Identification System, better known as AFIS, might produce something. After placing the stovepipe in the trunk of his car, he headed back to Perryville as he contemplated his next move.

Meanwhile, Jacob and Martha had delivered hamburgers and soft drinks to their neighbors but mentioned nothing about the abandoned child found in their pumpkin patch. They dined in silence and gave their attention to Willy and Dusty. Afterward Jacob built a fire in the fireplace and Martha busied herself connecting portable chargers and mobile devices.

By the time Martha went upstairs to change into Buffalo plaid flannel pajamas and heavy wool socks and returned with several top sheets and pillows, the light was fading. Jacob had rearranged the sectional couch so that it now was positioned directly in front of the fire at a safe distance.

As she covered the sofa with the sheets, she asked Jacob, "Can you grab some blankets from the linen closet?"

Dressed in sweatpants and a long-sleeved medium weight thermal crew shirt, he came back down the stairs carrying a stack of blankets, placing them on a corner of the sofa.

Now moving only by firelight, Martha found the utility lighter and lit the multiple wicks of a large pillar candle in an equally large and thick blown glass lantern staged in a corner of the living room. Under other circumstances, it would have set the mood for a romantic candlelight dinner. Instead, it was simply another soft light source.

Jacob reclined in one the corner of the gray sectional, the cats beside him. He grabbed Martha's hand as she started to sit on the adjoining section.

"We just need sleep, Martha."

She withdrew her hand from his grasp and curled

up in the corner opposite him. "I agree, but it's not going to fix it."

It, he surmised, was the abandoned child. "I can't fix this, Martha."

"I can pretend you can."

Without hesitation he responded, "No, you can't."

The ensuing silence dragged on for so long he thought she had fallen asleep. His comfort with that thought was shattered when she said, "Tell me, Jacob. Why did you never tell me you possess a sixth sense?"

Baffled, he said, "A what?"

"That's how Harriet Johnson described your knowing that tragedy was going to strike in Principio Furnace this morning. She said your mother had . . . what were her words . . . oh, yes, a 'powerful sixth sense.'"

Frustrated, Jacob drew his hand down his face in a gesture to wash away the emotion. "There is no logical connection between finding an abandoned child and obeying procedural law and you wanting to pretend that I can fix it," he said. "I can't fix it. No more than I can control when I get a feeling that something—good or bad—is about to happen. It just happens."

When she offered no rebuttal, he sighed and added. "If I get a feeling, as I did this morning, and there is a possibility that other people are in danger then I will, if possible, take action."

Her eyes narrowed and he would have sworn, even in the dim firelight, he could see daggers being thrown from them in his direction. He got up, drew open the fireplace screen and used tongs to shift the positions of logs before adding a new piece of firewood to the stack.

"And, Martha, I know why you demanded this morning that everyone agree to a standardized message about the timing of events. It's covered and it will not jeopardize our being foster parents."

As he closed the screen, Martha said, "Is that another sixth sense?"

He reclaimed his sleeping spot next to the cats, and said, "No, Martha. It's trust." The only sound that followed Jacob's final words was the popping and crackling of burning wood.

6

Life Moving Ahead

SEVEN HOURS LATER JACOB WOKE WHEN he felt the enormous weight of the youngest and heaviest cat, shorthaired Dusty with his patches of different shades of brown fur and white paws, walking across his torso. Willy, the amber-eyed Russian Blue, thinner, older, and wiser, simply had the grace to meow in his face. Martha was still tucked in the opposite side of the sectional, buried under her special acrylic blanket decorated with whales, her right foot habitually uncovered and exposed like a thermostat. She was snoring softly, something she repeatedly denied doing, even when confronted with audio evidence.

Jacob nudged Dusty, whom he had come to refer to as Breadbox, until the Ragdoll Siamese mix with piercing blue eyes jumped down and landed on the floor with a definite thud. Picking up Willy, Jacob carried him toward the kitchen, pausing only to snuff out the candle. One of the three wicks still had a slight flicker.

As Jacob stepped over the threshold into the kitchen, he put Willy down on the vinyl plank floor and as he habitually did, automatically reached out and switched on the overhead lights. The instant illumination surprised him and he sent up a prayer of thanks to PIW Utilities. He hoped power had been safely restored to other areas of Principio Furnace.

After feeding the cats, he checked his and Martha's cell phones. No missed local calls, but there were several from out of state. Not surprisingly, most were on Martha's phone. She would be disappointed that Dr. Howard had not called and he sincerely hoped there would be a call from the good doctor this morning.

He also checked the local weather forecast, relieved to see the temperature forecast didn't include wind or rain. The ambient temperature was predicted to be a nice 48 degrees Fahrenheit. It was certainly several degrees cooler than yesterday.

He put down the phone and followed his normal routine as the early riser, starting Martha's morning coffee. Every morning, with few exceptions, she had a hot, steaming cup of Seattle's Best Coffee Post Alley Blend. It was a passion and a routine he didn't share. He didn't even like the smell of coffee.

Jacob desperately wanted to jump into a very hot shower and wash away the thick layer of stress that clung to his skin like dust did to a piece of furniture. At that moment he, quite selfishly, could think of nothing else.

It was unlikely that he or anyone else in Principio Furnace or surrounding areas would ever forget the events of yesterday. It began with a freak tornado and, for him and Martha, ended in the discovery of an abandoned child. He knew today Martha would be anxious about the child and would insist on contacting Dr. Howard. Given what Jacob deemed a ridiculous spat with Martha at the end of the day, he wasn't sure he was ready to have a conversation about it with her today or any day in the future. He could be as obstinate as Martha.

Before racing up the stairs to enjoy a shower, he closed the fireplace flue and gazed once more at his sleeping wife. For the moment she appeared at peace; there was no frown, no furrowed brow. As he started up the stairs, he could smell her coffee brewing and knew she could too.

Martha certainly smelled the coffee, her nostrils tingled in anticipation. She desperately wanted a cup, but waited until she heard the shower running before rising. She folded the blanket and then walked into the kitchen, but there was no bounce in her step in celebration for the beginning of a new day, a fresh start.

Before pouring a cup of coffee, she bent down and stroked both cats between their ears and then moaned in satisfaction with the first sip of the dark brew. She picked up her mobile phone and then Jacob's to review missed calls. Her heart sank like a lead balloon when finding no call from Dr. Howard on either phone. A knot of anxiety grew in her stomach remembering how the doctor had promised to call and didn't.

There were many calls and text messages from friends and family across the country and she wondered why she hadn't heard the mobile phones ring. Suspicious, she checked the phone's settings and discovered Jacob had not only turned off phone notifications but also had muted call volume on her phone and on his. Despite knowing his motivation likely was to ensure they both got some uninterrupted and much needed sleep; his actions nonetheless were a source of irritation.

Unlike Jacob, she hadn't slept well. It wasn't just their late night spat that put her brain in overdrive. She wasn't ready to admit she was being irrational and, yes, childish, in demanding he fix what was unfixable. Having lost a child, first to a tragic car accident, and then to a miscarriage, she struggled to come to terms emotionally and intellectually with how anyone could deliberately abandon a child. She had an equally hard time understanding how anyone could do the same with an animal.

Even if a parent was trying to protect their child from a dangerous situation, surely there had to be more viable and better options than leaving a child in a pumpkin patch. Safe Haven Laws might apply to infants, but she had to, wanted to, believe any church, hospital, fire station, and police station had the moral obligation to take appropriate actions to protect any child left anonymously at their location. If there were criminal laws that could be attached to whomever abandoned a child, then that should be a secondary priority, not the first.

Last night, as she did every night, she expressed gratitude for the blessings in her life. Martha gave thanks for the good health and safety of her husband, her friends and family, her neighbors, and the community of Principio Furnace. She also prayed for the child she and Jacob had found.

And the immense stress of yesterday's events opened an old wound. The death of her husband and child many years before punched a hole in her universe that left her numb. She buried her husband, buried her child, and then buried that chapter in her life. It took more than a year of counseling to work through her grief and some deep soul searching before she relocated to another state and started a new life. A life she eventually chose to share with Jacob.

Other than revealing she had been married, and her husband and child had been killed in a car accident with a drunk driver, Martha shared no details about her past life with Jacob. She wanted no shadows, no comparisons. She wanted fresh. And the child they found yesterday deserved a fresh start. It was critical to guard the welfare of the child and protect his emotional, physical, mental, and spiritual health.

She wasn't ready to return calls. Instead, she sent a group text message to friends, another to family. Each was the same. She and Jacob were safe, little damage to the house, none to the farm, but that the experience was very frightening and there were members of the community who were suffering. She included a promise to call everyone when she was able. And she deliberately withheld any information about finding a child abandoned in their pumpkin patch.

No longer hearing the shower running, Martha sat on the chair before the small built-in desk tucked in an alcove in the kitchen and opened the laptop. She Googled Principio Furnace and found it trending on Facebook and Bluesky with news about the tornado. Skipping both social media platforms, she focused on scanning local news sites. There were many articles about the tornado, some short interviews, some longer, and only one reference to a child found and no mention of where.

Martha was still scrolling through articles with her large cup of coffee on a Keep Calm and Carry On stone coaster Jacob gave her last Christmas. Jacob found her sitting in front of the computer sitting in a position he found extremely peculiar. He once described Martha's strange sitting position to a friend who said it sounded like a "royal ease" position. According to his friend, it was a variation of an Indian religious position where the left leg was bent and the foot resting at the same level as the seated body. The right foot dangled freely toward the floor. He always wondered where Martha picked up the strange habit.

She knew Jacob was standing behind her because she smelled the body wash and the soft fragrance of the shampoo he used. Barely turning her head, she glanced over her left shoulder saying, "Good morning."

He placed his hands on her shoulders, gently squeezed, and said, "Morning," before asking, "Did you sleep well?"

"Yes," she lied, and then without pausing added, "No calls from Dr. Howard."

"I know," he said, moving into the kitchen and pulling a carton of large brown eggs out of the refrigerator. Then he declared with a confidence she didn't share, "She'll call."

Pressing forward, she said, "Aside from the Cecil Courier, no other paper had a picture of the boy. It's a single picture with a tag line that reads, 'Do you know this child? Call the Perryville police department.' The number is listed below."

She noted that he was dressed in heavy jeans and an old baseball team sweatshirt, as he would if he planned to work in the fields.

"Would you like a scrambled egg with cheese?" Jacob asked, showing no interest in what she had just said.

Martha said, "Yes," and then asked her question, unable to suppress a note of irritation in her voice. "Don't you think it odd that more media aren't covering the fact that an abandoned child was found?"

Martha's annoyance didn't escape him. Still, he didn't offer an emotional reaction. Quite the contrary.

In a voice that was unnaturally flat, Jacob said, "I'm sure Chief Cox fulfilled his obligations and notified the appropriate state child welfare agencies and media outlets as prescribed by law. He doesn't strike me as a man who abandons his responsibilities. Chief Cox can't control what the media does and doesn't post." He handed her a plate of scrambled eggs, cheese melted on top, with toast. He also set a glass of freshly squeezed orange juice down next to the laptop.

Jacob took a seat at the table. Martha joined him.

"What's the plan today?"

"Hmmm, we won't be lollygagging."

The sound of Martha's fork dropping on the plain white porcelain pierced the silence. Her arms flung out, hands up and brows wrinkled, Martha repeated, "We won't be what? Lollygagging? Is that some fishermen term you learned when you were in a longliner fishing boat cruising the Bering Sea around the Aleutian Islands chasing after schools of Pacific cod?"

Unmoved by her mockery and theatrical display, he repeated calmly, "Lollygagging."

"Pray tell, what is lollygagging?"

"According to Mrs. Rittenhouse," he raised his voice ever so slightly, emphasizing her name as if it was in all caps, "It means don't be idle. Or in simpler terms, don't waste time."

"As if we could."

"Remember Steven is coming to clean up debris around the Johnson and Greyson properties along with ours. We'll see what we can do to help others in the community as well."

Martha's head snapped to attention when Jacob's phone rang. He clearly understood the look she sent him.

He answered her unspoken question with a shake of his head, saying, "Good morning, Steven. No, I'm ready. Martha has been waiting for the hot water to refresh before taking her shower. Thanks, but no, we've just had breakfast. Check with Patsy.

She may want something from Mickey D. See you when you get here."

Disappointed that the call wasn't from Dr. Howard, Martha had cleared the table and started to wash the dishes.

"Steven will be here in twenty minutes," Jacob said as pulled on work boots and then moved the living room furniture back into place.

"I'll go shower," Martha said, placing the last plate in the dish drying rack. She snatched her phone off the table and watched Jacob pick up Willy who was meowing at his feet and cradle him in his arms. Dusty, true to pattern, raced ahead of her on the stairs. The cat stopped every two steps in front of her, refusing to move forward until she scratched his back. His demand for her attention made her smile.

Miles away Chief Ken Cox pulled up in front of the brick building that served as headquarters for the Perryville Police Department. He was anxious to get to work and discover who had abandoned a child in a pumpkin patch and why.

Striding into the station's lobby he was once again debating about the addition of *Spathiphyllum* plant, commonly known as a peace lily, sitting at one end of a nearly five-foot long counter. Behind the counter sat Officer Georgia Straah, the woman who recently introduced the plant into the workspace, claiming the area needed to look less sterile.

A member of the force for three years, the mixed-race female was on the phone when he entered. He greeted her with a smile and a good morning and then walked into his office directly behind her.

Down the hall to his right, past some desks and chairs, was a door with a combination biometric and standard key lock for physical security. Beyond that door was a windowless room with four independent cells set off by floor to ceiling iron bars that served as holding areas. It was a small but serviceable temporary area that protected area citizens from an assortment of suspected law breakers.

When the call ended, Georgia stood, grabbed the clipboard with the locking arched rings off, and walked into the chief's office and handed it to him. She took up a position in the doorway with her thumbs tucked in her waistline.

He sat in a vintage swivel banker's chair behind a heavily scarred wooden desk that according to town historians had served the department for decades. Unlike his predecessor whose girth comfortably filled the chair, Chief Cox had the build of a runner. His body filled the chair with his weapon on and he still had room to spare.

He spoke first as he scanned the log, but he already knew the answer.

"Any calls come in about the child?"

At 11 p.m., he had called Chuck Duncan who

had been on duty and was told there had not been any calls about the child. Although he hoped for a different answer, it didn't surprise him.

"According to the log, no," she answered.

"Chuck said the only calls that came in were from people asking questions about Principio Furnace. As my Aunt Polly used to say, it's a mess," and his face reflected the grimness of his words.

Georgia, 36 and divorced, was herself an ex-vet who served in the Army as an MP. That credential on her resume shocked many. People young and old thought the statuesque beauty with her oblong face with high cheek bones and shapely lips should be walking a runway instead of an occasional beat in Perryville.

Georgia was trained to spot the signs of emotional suppression, even when done in the name of security. She saw the tightening of the chief's jaw, the flash of anger in his eyes.

"From the picture, the child is very young. Maybe 16 months old. Is that where the child was found? In Principio?"

"Yes. More specifically in a pumpkin patch at the Biddle Farm. Something that I don't want shared with any one," he cautioned, accenting his words as he locked eyes with her.

"Understood, sir."

Moving on, he asked if there had been a fax from

the forensic lab where he had dropped off the stove-pipe the night before.

"You know, I think I recall hearing a fax coming in when I was on the phone. Let me go check."

Minutes later she returned with two sheets of paper. Partial prints were found. The fact none matched any prints in AFIS didn't surprise him. He was sure a member of the boy's family had left the child at the Biddle Farm.

He picked up the phone and was about to call Dr. Howard when Georgia took an incoming call.

"It's Nick Barrett."

Surprising Georgia, he moaned and said, "Put him through."

7

It Began with
Mr. Rocky the Rooster

"M r. Barrett," answered Chief Cox. "Is she . . .?"

"You come lock her up, Chief," the farmer cut him off. He was bellowing. "She just hit at my granddaughter. My 10-year-old granddaughter! Do something now."

"I'll be right there, Mr. Barrett," and he hung up.

He quickly picked up his car keys and hat and told Georgia as he charged out the front door, "Look back at one of the citations issued to Mrs. Anderson. Maybe there's a name of a family member listed. Send it to me."

"Will do, sir," Georgia called back as she began typing the name, Anderson, launching a search in the citation database.

The sheriff backed out of his parking space, turned on his flashers, and sped down the road to Nick Barrett's property north of town.

In the job for a year, Ken Cox had earned a reputation for being fair and compassionate and choosing to issue citations for violations of the law instead of making arrests. The only person known to have objected vehemently to Chief Cox was the widow Mrs. Rose Bender Anderson.

After receiving more than 25 complaints over the summer, and discovering a history of complaints dating back three years, Chief Cox just days before had approached the city prosecutor, seeking his support in procuring a court order to confiscate the widow's BB gun. With the prosecutor's support, the sheriff met with Judge Foreaker, who also was familiar with the hazard the 76-year-old widow posed to the community. The judge gave him the warrant to confiscate the weapon, and he intended to do just that. He didn't understand why the threat Mrs. Anderson presented to the community had not been addressed years before.

On several occasions the aged widow attempted to use a BB gun to kill Mister Rocky, the rooster owned by farmer Nick Barrett whose land was adjacent to hers because she objected to his morning cock-a-doodle-doo. But her viciousness evolved, and Mrs. Anderson started shooting anyone who dared to walk on the trail between her fence and that along Barrett farm. Because of Mrs. Anderson's failing eyesight, Nick Barrett himself and several dog walkers and their canines had become her victims.

Nick Barrett's call today was the last straw. Today, Ken wasn't going to treat the situation with kid gloves. He intended to take possession of both Mrs. Anderson and the infamous BB gun.

As he turned onto the road leading to the home of Nick Barrett, the sheriff radioed Georgia and instructed her to dispatch Officer Chuck Edmondson to the home of Rose Anderson, and to advise him to park a mile away from the woman's residence. "I'll make contact with Officer Edmonson after I take a statement from Mr. Barrett."

At the end of the driveway to the Barrett Farm was a huge white two-story house with a green front door and a wrap-around porch. A wreath made of colorful fall leaves adorned the door, and pumpkins of varying sizes, some carved, some not, decorated the porch.

Beyond the house, he could see a large red barn and cows roaming about. And he knew that somewhere there were chickens. Lots of them. Barrett organic brown eggs were sold throughout the state.

On the front porch stood several people—at least one woman and several children of varying ages—watching him approach. At the bottom of the stairs stood Nick Barrett, whom Ken had met on at least two other occasions. Standing beside Nick were his twin sons, clearly his mirror images. It wasn't hard to see the family resemblance. All three were tall, sturdy men with a round faces, fleshy noses, and surprisingly thin lips set so tightly that Ken wondered if their square jaws hurt. And all three were dressed alike—blue jeans, flannel shirts, canvas jackets, rubber boots, and baseball caps.

Ken got out of the cruiser and greeted the men. Nick introduced his sons as Addison and Emerson.

Pointing to the man standing to his left, Nick said, "Emerson is the father of my granddaughter, Bella, who that *crazy* old woman shot today. Bella and my other grandchildren were playing a game of catch with Buddy, our dog. Turns out Addison's boy, Jordan, has quite an arm. The ball he threw landed on the trail, near Mrs. Anderson's front yard. Buddy ran after it. Bella followed. We heard . . ."

Emerson cut off his father, "And then we heard my daughter scream. I found her on the ground, clutching her left eye. Mrs. Anderson was standing over her holding that BB gun and sputtering that she hadn't meant to hit the child."

"I disarmed her," announced Addison, "while Emerson picked up Bella."

"Please bring the gun to me," said Chief Cox, giving Addison Barrett his full attention. The young man turned on his heels and went up the stairs, past the silent observers, and into the house.

"Where's Bella?" Ken asked.

"At the hospital emergency room with her mother and grandmother," Emerson answered.

"Did the metallic pellet strike her in the eye?" Ken hoped the answer was no.

"We're waiting to hear," said the senior Barrett, and his phone rang just as Addison reappeared with the BB gun.

Ken opened the trunk to the cruiser, grabbed a pair of disposable gloves, and took the BB gun and placed it in the trunk.

"You'll have to come in and be fingerprinted, Addison, so we can eliminate your prints on the gun."

"Can it wait?"

"It can wait until Monday."

"Okay. I'll come in then."

Ken heard a cell phone ring, watched Nick pulled a phone from his pocket and say, "Midge" and watched the man rubbing the back of his neck, something Ken himself had been known to do on occasion.

The observers, all of whom Ken guessed were Barrett family members, descended the stairs. They stood behind the patriarch, and listening, as Ken did, to a one-sided conversation. "What did the doctor say?" Minutes passed and he finally said, "I'll tell Emerson and the others. And yes, Chief Cox is here," before ending the conversation.

Nick, still holding the phone, sighed and told everyone, "The pellet struck Bella in the eye," and when a communal moan went up, he held up his hand. "The emergency doctor said it appears the eye is just seriously bruised. But to be sure, they've called a pediatric ophthalmologist at Christiana Hospital in Newark and requested an emergency appointment. Out of precaution, Bella is being transported there now by ambulance."

Giving his attention to Chief Cox, Nick said, "My wife is on the way home. We'll be accompanying our son, Emerson, to Newark. Do you need us to file some paperwork because we definitely want to press charges against that woman?"

"Yes," affirmed Chief Cox, "I'll be filing criminal charges against Mrs. Anderson and arresting her. Did anyone take pictures of the where Bella was found?"

Addison piped up, "I did."

The sheriff pulled a business card out of his pocket and handed it to Addison. "Please send the images to the email address at the bottom. Any pictures of the child's injuries?"

"I'm sure my mother took some."

"Those too would be good to have."

"That's her car coming up the drive," Addison said, giving an upward nod to a Ford Passenger Wagon speeding toward them.

Ken turned as the vehicle came to a stop behind his cruiser. The woman who exited the car was aptly named. Compared to her husband and twin sons, she was tiny. But her sons clearly inherited the thickness and volume of her brown hair.

Like her husband and sons, she wore blue jeans and a plaid flannel shirt, and what appeared to be a light gray down vest. She made a beeline for Ken, right hand extended. He shook it and wasn't surprised by the firm grip.

Introducing herself, she said, "Good morning, I'm Midge Barrett."

He greeted her solemnly with a "Good morning, Mrs. Barrett. Sorry to meet you under these circumstances."

She added, "Tell me that you're going to arrest that wretched woman." Her brown eyes under slightly drooping lids were laser sharp and Ken returned her gaze.

"I am," he said, at which point she covered his hand with both of hers and said, "Bless you. Stop her from hurting anyone else."

When his hand was free, he pulled out another business card from his breast pocket, wrote his phone number across the back, and handed it to Mrs. Barrett. "That's my personal number. Please let me know your granddaughter's status after you see the specialist. And if you did take pictures of your granddaughter's injury, I'd like to add them as evidence in my criminal investigation. You can send them to the email address on the front."

The word "criminal" seems to reassure everyone that the Sheriff was going to take action. Nick climbed into the Ford's driver's seat, Emerson in the back, and Midge in the front passenger seat.

Addison called out, "Mom," and she offered her son a faint smile. Then extending her right arm out the window, she took his hand in hers and said, "I know. Look after everyone, Addison. You're in charge."

When Ken turned back to Addison, his right arm was wrapped around a young woman with two toddlers clinging to her legs. His left arm was wrapped around a teenage boy. It was hard to tell if the boy was Addison or Emerson's son, but they were definitely Barrett offspring.

Ken got back in his cruiser, rolled down his window, and said to Addison, "I'll be in touch."

He drove past the turn to the Anderson home and pulled off the road behind Officer Edmonson's patrol car. Stepping out, he knocked on the window and ushered the officer to step out.

"Good morning, Chuck."

"Mornin' sir."

"Before we approach Mrs. Anderson, I'm going to contact the person listed on one of the citations as a distant family relative. One Mr. John Anderson on Old Main Road in North East. Georgia found a current number."

Pulling out his mobile phone and setting it to speaker, the chief dialed the number.

A woman answered, with a simple "Hello."

"Hello," responded Ken, "This is Chief Ken Cox with the Perryville Police Department. Is there a Mr. John Anderson available?"

There was a long pause of silence and then a male voice answered, "This is John Anderson."

"Are you related to Rose Bender Anderson?"

Hesitating, he responded, "In a way."

"In what way?"

"She was married to my uncle, John. I'm named after him."

He exchanged a look with his officer. "Is there anyone with a closer relationship to Mrs. Anderson that you're aware of?"

"I honestly don't know much about Rose. She was my uncle's second wife."

Ken dropped his head down, disappointed that there was no one to assist Mrs. Anderson, and delivered the bad news. "I'm about to arrest Mrs. Anderson."

"Arrest?" The man's tone registered shock. "For what?"

"She shot a 10-year-old child with a BB gun."

"Dear Lord," retorted John. "Is the child okay?"

"The child is on her way to Christiana."

"She was injured?"

"The pellet apparently struck her in or near her left eye. A pediatric ophthalmologist has been called in and will see her when she arrives."

John Anderson sighed and said somberly, "So this is very serious."

"Extremely. I'll be taking her to the station and charging her with criminal mischief and other things. She'll also be fingerprinted. Then we'll set a time for her to appear before Judge Foreaker."

"She's not a young woman."

"No, she's not. I know she has problems with her eyesight, but I suspect she has other medical issues. I was holding out hope that someone could help her," he said with great sincerity.

More silence, and then, "There are some things I must attend to first. Will you delay taking her to the station until we can arrive?"

Without hesitating, Ken said, "Yes." Disconnecting, he looked at Officer Edmondson and said, "Now we wait."

"Check in with Georgia, Chuck, give her our location, fill her in with what's happening, and ask if she's received some images from Addison Barrett."

While Chuck was following his instructions, Ken grabbed a yellow legal pad and began writing notes about his interaction with members of the Barrett family. He saw the old silver Toyota Camry slow as it passed, and then watched as the driver did a U-turn and drove back and parked behind the cruiser.

Ken estimated that the burly man who got out of the car was in his 40s, very tan, and dressed very conservatively. He shook the man's hand, saying, "Thank you, Mr. Anderson, for coming."

"It's Pastor, Chief Cox. My wife and I have barely been back in the country, in Maryland, a week. We've were on a mission in the Congo for the last five years."

"Welcome home, Pastor. I'm glad you've come and I truly hope you can provide emotional assistance to Mrs. Anderson."

"I'll do my best."

"I think it would be best if you went ahead of us, Pastor."

"Okay." He got back in his car, turned it around, drove a mile, and then turned into the driveway leading to the Anderson home.

Chief Cox and Officer Edmondson followed. The Pastor and his wife were knocking on the door when they parked their cars. Both men exited their vehicles and watched. Rose Anderson opened the door and when she saw the man standing there, she covered her mouth with her hands.

"Rose," said the Pastor, who looked back at his wife for support. The woman, also in her forties, stepped forward and embraced Rose. Unlike her husband, the younger Mrs. Anderson was fair skinned, but also dressed conservatively.

When the two Mrs. Andersons entered the house, the Pastor turned and approached Chief Cox.

"I realize you have a duty to perform, Chief, but can you be persuaded to allow my wife and I to escort Rose to your station? Joyce, my wife, is helping Rose to gather some clothes and any medications she takes so that we can take her to our house and help her. I think there are some attorneys in our congregation that may be willing to provide legal assistance. We'll bring her back to Perryville for any court appearances."

Instead of responding immediately to the Pastor, Chief Cox addressed Officer Edmonson.

"Please head back to the station and prepare to do an ink and roll of fingerprints for Mrs. Anderson. I believe the digital system is currently down. I've entered the paperwork charging her with the criminal assault of a minor child. Print it out and make copies."

"Yes sir," answered the officer and returned to his car.

The sheriff waited until the patrol car pulled out before he answered the Pastor.

"I'm comfortable with that, Pastor. And I'm glad you're welcoming Mrs. Rose Anderson into your home. I take no pleasure in taking a 76-year-old woman to jail. But, she did break the law and injured a child who was doing nothing more than retrieving a ball a dog had chased after." He wanted to say more but didn't. He'd save it for the hearing.

"Have you heard any news about the child's condition?"

"Not yet."

Both Mrs. Andersons came out of the house. The younger woman was carrying a canvas bag and a set of keys, locking the door behind them. Rose Anderson carried a purse.

The sheriff stood next to the pastor's car. He reached out and opened the back door for Rose Anderson, saying, "Mrs. Anderson, I've agreed to allow your nephew and his wife to transport you to the police station. I am charging you with a criminal offense for inflicting serious bodily injury on a minor. Do you understand these charges, Mrs. Anderson?"

Her eyes dazed, she looked up at John Anderson and muttered "Yes."

"When we arrive at the station, Mrs. Anderson, your picture will be taken and you'll be finger-printed. Do you understand?"

She nodded, but Ken said, "I need to hear your answer, Mrs. Anderson."

She answered "Yes," and Ken closed the car door. He then made eye contact with the pastor, and said, "Sir, please follow me to the station." Moments later the sheriff was again traveling down the highway back to town, his eyes scanning the road ahead and frequently checking the rearview mirror. He wanted to make sure his assessment of John Anderson's character was accurate and the man was following him to the police station.

8

Follow-up

IT TOOK JUST UNDER AN HOUR to finish processing Mrs. Rose Anderson once they arrived at the station. On their departure, Georgia let out a heavy sigh and commented, "What a morning."

Back in his office, Georgia handed him a manila folder, the name Barrett printed in black on the middle tab. He opened it and looked at images of Bella Barrett on the ground, Bella Barrett being carried by her father Emerson, Bella Barrett in the emergency room at the hospital, Bella Barrett in an ambulance.

It was hard looking at the aftermath of the assault with a BB gun by Rose Anderson. It was equally hard remembering the woman who looked many years beyond her seventy-six years dressed in a wrinkled striped shirt and plaid skirt wearing mismatched socks and badly stained white tennis shoes with holes in the toes who wept as she was fingerprinted. His job was to enforce the laws and regulations. He also was charged in looking after Perryville's most vulnerable residents—one at the beginning of her life, the other potentially at the end of hers.

He was still looking at the pictures when his wife and daughter walked in, and he had just enough time to close the folder and put it in a drawer. His action didn't escape his wife's attention and when she shot him a questioning look, he silently mouthed the word, "later" in response.

His daughter, Meli, raced around the desk and nearly leapt in his lap. She grabbed his face between her tiny hands and planted a kiss on his mouth. "I miss you, Daddy."

Returning the kiss, he said, "I miss you too, baby girl."

"We brought lunch," said his wife, Alison. She smiled and held up a brown paper bag and set it on his desk. "A ham sub from Spence's."

"For one or for two?"

"For one. Meli has a play date at Bob's Pizza Hut with her cousins."

"You're going to eat pizza with Joey, Carla, and Sage?" She nodded yes.

"Without me?" He reached down and tickled his daughter's neck below her left ear. Squirming and giggling, she climbed off his lap.

Looking at her outfit of leggings in a floral print and a T-shirt hanging out under her jacket, Ken asked, "Did you dress yourself today, Meli?"

"She did," answered his wife, who was dressed in black leggings topped with a loosely knit light brown sweater that set off her hair color and blue eyes. Pulling out her phone and glancing at the time, she said hurriedly, "We have to go."

"I'll walk you out," Ken told her and swooped up a giggling Meli in his arms.

He eyed the brown bag on his desk when he returned and asked, "Georgia, have you eaten lunch?"

"No, I haven't."

"Would you like a ham sub from Spence's?"

Surprised, she answered, "Are you sure you don't want it?"

Dropping the bag on her desk, "Very sure. Enjoy."

Ever since Alison mentioned that she and Meli were going to have pizza, all he could think about was a vegetarian pizza, with no sauce, no onions, fresh tomatoes, thin crust. Putting his food craving aside, he resurrected the agenda he mentally laid out for himself as he drove into work. It was his intent to telephone Dr. Jill Howard and check the status of the child after a medical evaluation. He also wanted to discuss his findings at the Biddle Farm.

He made a single call to Dr. Howard. When there was no answer after multiple rings, he left a message with her after-hours service requesting a callback at her earliest convenience. Ten minutes later she called.

"Chief, are you calling about the boy?"

"I am, but can you do a face to face."

There was a slight hesitation and then she said, "I'm about to leave the hospital and go to my parent's in Port Deposit to pick up my children. Could you meet me in the lobby of the hospital?"

"I'll be there in ten minutes, Dr. Howard."

He could smell the oregano on the ham sub as he walked by Georgia's desk, and he felt a hunger pang. "I'll be at the hospital checking on the abandoned boy. Call me immediately if there's a call from a Barrett family member."

Jill Howard was seated in a corner of the lobby away from the main entry. Instead of a white lab coat with her name emblazoned across the pocket, she was wearing jeans and a blue wool jacket overtop a brightly colored blouse in an abstract design.

He approached her and she removed her large purse from the adjacent chair so he could sit.

"Good morning, Dr. Howard," he said as he sat. "Thanks for taking the time to meet with me."

"It's going to be short Chief Cox. As I said, I have to pick up my children and I've been up most of the night."

She did look fatigued. "Were you up all night because of the child?"

"With *a child*," she said with emphasis, "but not the one found in the Biddle Farm pumpkin patch. It's an infant with meningitis."

Alarmed, he said, "Meningitis? Meningitis can be deadly, can't it?"

"Yes, but I think we caught it in time. The child could be in the hospital for months. Usually children are vaccinated, but this child's family, sadly, doesn't believe in vaccinations. That belief nearly cost them the life of their child. Their only child."

Ken sent up a prayer that his daughter Meli was vaccinated. "And the boy the Biddle's found? Is he sick?"

"He is, but not with meningitis. With pneumonia." She put up a hand to stop any further questions. "And out of an abundance of caution, the child is isolated in the hospital until we know with certainty that his health is not at risk and he does not pose a risk to anyone else should some other medical issue pop up."

With that assurance, he asked, "Do the Biddles know?"

"No," and he detected a note of regret in her voice. "I promised I'd call last night, but circumstances . . . well, I couldn't. I didn't. I'll call them on my way to Port Deposit."

"Before you talk to them, there's something you should know," and he proceeded to tell her what he found at the Biddle Farm during his investigation.

MARTHA FELT BETTER AFTER SHOWERING, but before she joined Jacob and the others outside, she logged onto the farm's HostGator account and added a banner to the Biddle Farm webpage. In a boxed message, she expressed gratitude for all who offered assistance to the residents and businesses in the aftermath of an unprecedented weather event in Principio Furnace. Knowing that Jacob wanted to resume business as usual as soon as possible, she added that Biddle Farm would reopen as scheduled the next day.

When she went outside, she found Jacob walking around their property with the iPad snapping pictures. Moving behind him, Martha asked, "For insurance purposes?" as she pulled out work gloves tucked in the back pockets of her jeans.

Without turning he answered, "Yes. I've already taken pictures of Harriet and Earl's house and Clint and Patsy's. We can upload the pictures to cloud storage for both. For the Johnsons, we'll upload to Steven's cloud account." Martha wondered if any member of the Johnson or Greyson family saw the irony in Jacob diligently creating an historical record of damage to their houses resulting from the tornado he intuited.

Martha made her way across the back yards, picking up shingles as she went. She said hello to Harriet, Earl, and Steven, and took a small dog biscuit treat out of her right pocket for Jackson who was barking and running around her in circles. She even asked Steven if he was responsible for the heavy-duty 32-gallon containers that everyone was throwing shingles and other debris into.

She asked each person how they had gotten through the night without heat and electricity. She smiled when Harriet said she and Earl had snuggled together with Jackson in front of their fireplace. She and Jacob had done the same thing she told them with Willy and Dusty. It wasn't a lie she told herself. A half-truth, but not a lie.

Next, she crossed the lawn, stepping on and over shingles, to Clint and Patsy and asked how they fared. She learned they had ended taking the children to Linda, Clint's sister's house in Elk Neck and spent the night there.

"We left the twins at Linda's house for another night because we knew today would be clean up mode," Patsy told her.

"Good choice," said Martha, as she bent down and picked up more shingles and other debris. She found some of Harriet's Halloween decorations, broken and battered, in a back corner of the Greyson yard.

Picking up a few of the items, she gathered them in her arms and took them to Harriet. And then Martha emitted a moan when she spied pieces of the large old wooden bucket that she had filled with white chrysanthemums as part of their autumn decor and placed on her and Jacob's front porch just days before Halloween.

The moan drew Jacob's attention, and he called out, "What's wrong?"

Martha pointed to the bucket. He shrugged his shoulders and said, "I'm grateful that our houses are still standing. And, I'm grateful no one was injured."

"Amen," said Harriet. Earl echoed the sentiment.

Steven stopped gathering broken pieces of fencing scattered across the yards and came to stand next to his mother. Her gaze was fixed on the big white oak tree that dominated their back yard. Her stance with drooped shoulders and no sparkle in her usually bright eyes conveyed a deep sadness. Staring at the tree with multiple broken limbs, Harriet solemnly declared, "That tree was so-o-o-o beautiful."

Steven put on a smile of encouragement, pulled her into him with a one-armed hug, and squeezed gently. "It still is, Mom. I know an arborist, Mitch Roberts, over in Port Deposit. I'll ask him to come over and look at the tree. It may be scarred, but I don't know if it's lost. I realize there are broken limbs, and he may know someone in the Amish community, maybe in Oxford or Lancaster, that can suggest how to repurpose the tree. The Amish are talented woodworkers."

Martha, who was standing close enough to overhear the exchange, said enthusiastically, "That's a great idea, Steven."

Jacob, who bent to lift the broken limb that supported the rope swing with the faded and rusted red metal seat, asked, "What's a great idea?"

"Giving the oak tree a second chance," responded Martha.

"What does that mean?"

Mildly surprised, Martha asked, "Jacob, have you never read Shel Silverstein's *The Giving Tree*?"

Jacob's "Nope," drew similar comments from Harriet and Patsy.

Steven said, "It's great. Put it on his Christmas gift list, Martha."

"Will do," said Martha as she examined the downed limb. "It just needs a new source of support."

"We can do that." Steven's father, Earl, used the air as his drawing board. "A simple A-frame with a big, sturdy beam at the top. We could anchor the limb to it with some . . . oh, I don't know . . . some stainless-steel brackets or some iron."

"I think you're right, Dad," following his father's vision.

"It will serve the next generation of children in our small neighborhood," said Harriet, her eyes showed a spark of hope.

"I certainly like the idea," said Jacob, smiling.

"Preserving our childhood history."

"Wonderful," Patsy said gleefully.

Clint added, "Great idea. I like it."

"I'll make a new swing seat, and we can add the existing one—sadly it's rusted and unusable—to the new frame as a shelf or something," promised Steven.

"And paint the seat red, Steven," Patsy suggested.

Harriet, choking back a sob, "Son, you just made an awful day better. Thank you." Turning to look back at her neighbors, she extended the thank you to everyone, but her actions and next words had everyone's heads whipping around.

Color drained from Harriet's face, and she cried out, "Dr. Howard, Chief Cox. What's happened? Are my grandchildren all right? Carol?"

Jacob called out, "It's okay, Mrs. Johnson," and raised his hands, palms outward, in a calming gesture to stop her from leaping to the wrong conclusion. "They're here to talk to me and Martha." Martha instantly, as was her custom, moved beside Jacob to present a united front.

"Is this true?" Harriet asked clutching at her heart, and Dr. Howard answered, "Yes."

Now five pairs of eyes looked to Jacob and Martha for answers.

With a heavy sigh, Jacob said in resignation, "Let's all go inside our house. Everyone just as well learn now what happened yesterday that brings Dr. Howard and Chief Cox here."

For the second time in two days, people gathered in the Biddle home. They sat in the living room and pulled in chairs from the dining room. Martha offered refreshments to everyone and took a chair next to Jacob in front of the fireplace.

"When Martha and I went to check on the farm yesterday, she found a child abandoned in the pumpkin patch directly behind the produce stand."

Willy and Dusty, who had partially descended the stairs to see what was going on, turned and raced back to the sanctuary of the bedroom when there was a simultaneous and fairly loud barrage of questions, most of which started with the pronoun "what?" Martha stepped in saying, "Jacob drove me and the child, a boy, to see Dr. Howard at the hospital in Perryville. Dr. Howard called Chief Cox."

"The child remains in the hospital," said Dr. Howard. Speaking directly to Jacob and Martha, she explained there had been an emergency at the hospital the night before, which is why she didn't call them. "Today, we didn't get an answer when we called, which is why Chief Cox and I decided to come here directly."

"The boy," Martha asked anxiously, reaching for Jacob's hand. "Is he all right?"

"He has a touch of pneumonia, Martha, so we're

keeping him in the hospital."

"For how long?" Martha asked, to which Dr. Howard answered, "Maybe a few days, Martha."

"Are you here Chief Cox because someone came forward and identified the child," Jacob asked.

"No one came forward, Mr. Biddle," answered Ken Cox.

"Call me Jacob."

"Jacob."

"Did you find something in the pumpkin patch?" Jacob asked, sensing the chief was hesitant to share what he discovered with everyone in the room. "Chief, everyone here may not be able to claim a bloodline, but we are, by choice, family. I trust everyone in this room to guard whatever information you share."

"I examined your pumpkin patch. The boy was placed there deliberately."

Shocked, Jacob said, "What?"

Horrified by his statement, Martha spoke out, "No. You must be mistaken."

"I'm not," he answered, his voice flat and firm, meeting her gaze.

Patsy asked quietly, "What did you find, Ken."

Shifting his attention to Patsy, Ken answered her. "The boy was, as Mrs. Biddle described it, seated on a block of peat moss next to a section of stovepipe. The stovepipe was some piece of debris that landed in the pumpkin patch because of the tornado. It was deliberately placed near the peat moss, driven into the ground so that it would catch the attention of, I suspect, Jacob or Martha Biddle."

Continuing, he said, "There's a spot in the woods at the rear of the patch where someone sat and watched until the boy was discovered."

Patsy spoke up, "I'm sure you submitted the pipe for forensics, Ken. Did you get any prints off it?"

"None that matches anyone in AFIS."

"What's AFIS?" asked Martha.

"It stands for Automated Fingerprint Identification System. It's primarily a database of biometric fingerprints. It was initially used by the FBI, but law enforcement everywhere now has access to it."

"Are you saying that we were targets?" Jacob said.

"Yes, I am."

With this pronouncement, a silence fell in the room, interrupted only by the ringing of the chief's cell phone.

9

Plans Change

CHIEF COX STEPPED OUT ONTO THE porch to take his call and Jacob waited just a moment before saying, "Patsy . . ."

"Yes, Jacob, I believe him," she answered the question before he fully formed it.

"So do I, Jacob," Dr. Howard spoke up.

Exasperated, Martha asked, "Why would anyone target us?"

Leaning forward and dropping her clutched hands between her knees, Patsy said, "You and Jacob are perfect targets. You're young, own a home, a business, and appear to be financially secure. Both of you are active in and respected by the community."

Neither Martha nor Jacob knew how to respond to her statement, especially when Harriet and Earl agreed with her. So did Dr. Howard. Clint and Steven just listened.

Speculating, Patsy asked, "The child you found.

Are you interested in fostering him?"

Martha didn't hesitate to say, "Yes."

Jacob's response was more reserved. "Everyone in this room, except maybe Steven, knows Martha and I have completed the necessary steps to become foster parents."

"I knew," said Steven, and there was no need for him to reveal who told him."

"It's okay, Steven," Martha said, disappointed that Jacob didn't simply answer yes. "You're family, and Stovepipe Peat is going to need a family." As an afterthought, she added, "At least temporarily."

Perplexed, Harriet asked, "Who is Stovepipe Peat?"

"The child found in the pumpkin patch," Dr. Howard explained. "That's how Martha referred to him when she and Jacob brought him into the hospital." Harriet appeared to process the information.

Curious, Steven asked, "Say, are you talking about the child pictured in the Cecil Whig online this morning? The one with an explosion of dark curls?"

Jacob nodded yes, and seeing Chief Cox at the front door, jumped up and quickly crossed the room to let him back in.

"Sorry for the interruption," Chief Cox said and glancing around the room, realized between his exit and reentry something had changed. Everyone was sitting perfectly still and no one was smiling. He looked to Patsy Armour Greyson and Dr. Howard hoping for an answer. It was his fellow member of law enforcement who gave him one.

"I suggested some reasons Martha and Jacob could have been targeted," Patsy said, and gave him a quick summary.

"All true," the chief agreed, "and I'd add another reason." Staring at Martha and Jacob, "You're both healthy."

"So true," said Dr. Howard.

"There's one more reason," offered Martha, surprising everyone.

"What's that?" asked Chief Cox. And then Martha Biddle, looking pale and her voice weak and flat, said what he wanted to, but couldn't.

"We're currently childless."

It was Dr. Howard who shattered the silence by saying, "Yes, that's true. But I believe if you had a child and found that boy abandoned in your pumpkin patch, you'd still pursue becoming a foster parent. It's just who you and Jacob are, Martha."

"Unless someone comes forward and explains the motivation for abandoning the child in your pumpkin patch, we can only speculate," interjected the chief, with a final warning. "I will, however, suggest you be hypervigilant. People could have been watching you both and probably still are."

Locking eyes with Jacob, he added, "I would encourage you to expand your electronic surveillance at the farm and," glancing around the room, "here at your home. Someone who works for you or who is connected to someone who works for you, or someone who makes deliveries to the farm. Someone," he emphasized the word, "someone knows who the boy is."

Standing, Chief Cox announced somberly, "There's a matter at the station that requires my attention." Then adopting a friendlier tone, he said, "It was a pleasure to meet you Mr. and Mrs. Johnson, and you, too, Steven. And Clint, I'm glad to have finally met you." Shifting his focus to Martha and Jacob, he told them to call him if they had any questions or the sense they were being watched.

Dr. Howard also rose, pulling her jacket down toward her waistline. "I, too, have to go. Martha, Jacob. Give me a few days to update you about the boy's condition." Smiling slightly, she added, "And I encourage you to begin child proofing your home, starting with adding a locking child gate at the top of the stairs and childproof locks on doors."

Martha said nothing, but she accompanied Jacob as he escorted Dr. Howard and Chief Cox to their cars, thanking them for personally delivering information to them. When they walked back into their house, everyone was cleaning up, putting chairs back in the dining area, loading glasses in the dishwasher.

"Thank you everyone," said Martha, forcing a smile as she tightly gripped the top of one of the ladder-back dining chairs.

Jacob, sensing her tension, did what he often did. He stood behind her and gently massaged her shoulders. She reached backed and removed his hands. He said nothing, but she heard the backdoor door close as he stepped outside.

Martha moved to the living room and sat in the corner of the sofa she had tried to sleep in the night before. She covered her eyes with the heels of her hands, pressing back the tears. Then she dragged her hands down her cheeks until her fingers reached her lips. Pulling her hands into fists, she let the tears flow. Once again, she felt Jacob had been less than supportive, and that revelation tore at her heart.

Startled when she heard Patsy yell "Martha!" from the back door, Martha stiffened and immediately stopped crying.

Patsy called out again, "Martha, lock the front door and grab your purse. We're all taking a break from clean up and going to the Crab House in North East for food."

When Patsy didn't get a response, she moved through the kitchen and found Martha seated in the corner of the sectional. Coming to standing in front of her, she asked, "Are you okay?"

"Yes, but go ahead without me. There are phone calls from yesterday I need to return."

Patsy put her hands on her hips and said, "No."

Astonished, Martha snapped, "Excuse me?"

"No, we're not going without you. You need to have a good meal, to relax, and take time to shake off Jacob's stupidity."

Martha said nothing, but Patsy did.

"Martha, it's clear Jacob's responses to Ken's questions and statements upset you, hurt you. Is Jacob stupid, ignorant, or selfish? Honestly, I don't know. Call it what you want. Unlike you, he really doesn't know the first thing about parenting."

She felt the hot rush of temper ripple through her body, spawned by Patsy's last remark. It was true, Jacob didn't have firsthand experience as a parent, and he often thoroughly annoyed her with his insensitive comments. Still, she knew in her heart that Jacob would be a good parent. Martha told herself she wouldn't have married him if she believed otherwise.

Martha reined in her anger and breathed deeply and slowly to calm herself and checked her instinct to respond swiftly and harshly to Patsy's remarks. She stood slowly, met Patsy's stare, and said, "Thank you for your concern. I'll just go tell Jacob I'm not going. I have calls to return," and she stepped around Patsy, went outside, and did just that. Patsy stepped out behind her.

When Martha went back inside, she grabbed her cell phone. Scrolling through the list of missed calls, she pressed the number for Rachel. It rang only once when the familiar voice said, "Marty! We've been worried sick. Are you okay?"

Hearing the soft, melodious voice of her best friend on the opposite coast, Martha assured her she was fine and began to tell her about the anxiety experienced by her and many others during the last two days. She deliberately left out the fact that Jacob was, according to his lifelong neighbors, a "sensitive" who foresaw the tornado and warned of its impending arrival.

She recounted the strange and bizarre events that contributed to unprecedented levels of stress for the community of Principio Furnace and for her personally. She told Rachel about finding a child abandoned in the pumpkin patch behind the market and his strange birth mark.

Martha ended the call with Rachel and made other calls to friends who had reached out to her. She was still returning those phone calls when Jacob walked back into the house two hours later.

She recognized the takeout box from the Crab House that Jacob dropped on the table in front of her and ended her last call, promising to call her friend back within the next two days. Jacob walked behind her, hugged her from behind by extending his right arm across her chest and grabbing her left shoulder, and planted a kiss on the top of her head. Martha popped the lid and smiled when she saw two fat crab cakes sitting on a small nest of coleslaw. "Thank you, Jacob."

Taking a bite, she asked, "Where is everyone?"

"Regrouping outside. Do you want to rejoin them?"

"Not before we have a conversation about the exchange this morning with Chief Cox and Dr. Howard."

Puzzled, Jacob said, "What about it?"

"How committed are you, Jacob, to fostering a child?"

"What do you mean?"

"I think the question is quite clear."

Irritated, Jacob said, "We've had long discussions about the subject. We've completed all the required paperwork. Passed all the background checks, interviews, and home inspections. So why are you questioning me now?"

"Because today when asked if you wanted to foster the child we found in the pumpkin patch, you didn't say yes. In fact, you seemed very reluctant to commit to fostering the child."

Patsy had warned him that Martha was upset. Admittedly, he was conflicted about fostering and couldn't say why.

"You're wrong," he said adamantly, his jaw set in a rigid line. "Dead wrong."

"Am I, Jacob? So you don't care about the color of the boy's skin, his heritage?"

Offended, Jacob said, "I really can't believe you're asking me those questions."

"Until today, Jacob, I didn't think I had to."

"And until today, Martha, I never thought you'd ask me such a question," he fired back.

She grabbed the box of crab cakes and placed it in the refrigerator.

"Tell me, Martha, what would you say . . . no, what would you do if I told you I didn't want the child abandoned in the pumpkin patch."

There wasn't even a moment of hesitation. In a cold, flat voice, Martha said, "I'd leave you."

Stunned, Jacob repeated, "You'd leave me?"

"Not just leave you, Jacob. I'd divorce you."

He could only stare at her, genuinely shocked by her words. "You're joking."

"Not at all."

"Do you remember the prenups we signed before we were married?"

"Of course I do."

"Then you'll remember that my personal financial resources are such that I could walk out the front door, find a new home, pay cash for it, and still never have to work another day in my life. You should also remember my telling you at that time, in front of our attorneys, that I was madly in love with you, wanted to marry you, but I needed to be assured you were committed to having a family."

"I do remember. I also remember giving you that assurance."

"Then what happened, Jacob, because today you abandoned that commitment to me."

He hung his head and said, "That wasn't my intention, Martha."

"It may not have been your intention, Jacob, but it was the result."

"Martha, I . . ." he started, only to have her cut him off.

Martha raised her hand, "Please stop, Jacob. I really have had quite enough for today, except to say that Chief Cox was wrong when he said we were targeted. We weren't. We were chosen."

She slipped back into her insulated vest, and then grabbed her phone, car keys, and purse from the built-in computer alcove. "I'm going to the store. The church sent out a request for items for the food bank."

Moving toward her, Jacob said, "I can go with you, Martha."

"I prefer you don't. The only thing I want from you, Jacob, is for you to honor you original commitment," she told him, pausing as she opened the front door. "And I would like a promise that if you decide to recommit, that any child that becomes part of our life, through fostering, adoption, or biologically will not ever carry a label of any one of those terms. Any child that is ours will simply be introduced as a gift from God."

When she closed the door, it was Jacob's turn to sit down and weep.

ON HIS WAY BACK TO PERRYVILLE, Ken pulled off the road at the Biddle Farm produce stand and called his favorite pizzeria. He stopped only long enough to place a to-go order for the vegetarian pizza topped with fresh tomatoes he'd been craving for hours. He was carrying his boxed meal when he walked into the station less than thirty minutes later.

Georgia was just finishing a call so he just gave a one-handed wave as he went by and entered his office. The call he had taken at the Biddles was from Nick Barrett, providing an update on the medical condition of his granddaughter. Ken had written down the words Nick used to describe what the doctor said about the ocular injury.

He went to the Internet and searched for information about a corneal abrasion, hyphema, and ended up having more questions than answers. With a sigh, he decided he needed an in-person session with an ophthalmologist and placed a call to Christiana Hospital.

10

Promises and Boundaries

Rᴇᴛᴜʀɴɪɴɢ ꜰʀᴏᴍ ʟᴜɴᴄʜ ʀᴇꜰʀᴇꜱʜᴇᴅ ᴀɴᴅ ready to again tackle cleanup activities, everyone gathered in the Biddle yard waiting for Jacob and Martha to join them after delivering takeout to Martha who had stayed home to return phone calls. While waiting, they assessed the cleanup progress made earlier and talked about contacting their individual insurance companies and identifying potential contractors to repair the roofs and chimneys. Clint indicated one of his dental patients owned a construction company and he'd reach out to him the next day to get some information. Steven said he, too, could root out the names and numbers of some contractors through his employer.

The group was just beginning a discussion about other needed property repairs when distracted by the sound of a car engine turning over. Moving to the south side of the Biddle house, they watched Martha drive away in her SUV toward Route 7. Surprised, Patsy turned and marched toward the back door of the Biddle house. Halfway there, her 5-foot-9-inch tall husband, Clint, who in his youth was a body-builder, blocked her way.

"I heard you tell Jacob during lunch about Martha being upset," her husband said in a tone of admonishment that she rarely heard from him.

"But," she said defensively, "I'm his friend . . ."

"And his friend should know when to allow him to work out his own problem." Then in a strong measured tone said, "Do. Not. Interfere."

She felt the punch of his words. Frowning, she fixed her gaze on the back door to the Biddle house, hoping Jacob would step out. He didn't.

Jacob felt as if he was having an emotional breakdown, a first for him. Until today, he never doubted himself, never questioned his motivations, his actions. He had explored occupations—trig-gered by something he saw, something he heard, something he read—not necessarily to accumulate wealth, but to acquire experience and to expand his knowledge base.

If an idea, a thought, a sense of an impending event, popped into his head, the origin of which he couldn't always define or explain, he followed it like it was some sort of treasure map. That's what happened yesterday, and he knew that disaster was going to strike Principio Furnace. And he had to take action to save others.

There was no question that Martha was his equal. But he had never before questioned whether *he* was her equal. She challenged him intellectually, spiritually, and emotionally. Politics, nationally and globally, was a frequent battleground. Although they had different perspectives, they managed to put aside those differences and find common ground. Both were fully committed to protecting the environment, human and animal rights, and supporting charities that defended all.

In his youth, Jacob had been inspired to seek out a job as a deckhand on a 144-foot crabber by watching documentaries about crab fishing in the Bering Sea. His parents voiced concerns but still supported his decision. Commercial fishing in Alaska had proved more challenging than he anticipated and was extremely dangerous. It was indeed a deadly occupation for many. A misstep could result in death and he, by the grace of God, had avoided what others had not.

Jacob had survived the grueling seasonal challenges on the often savage seas in Alaska. He also had worked on a longliner, which was slightly less hazardous than being a deckhand on a crabber. But it wasn't unusual for the season to be marked by the death of one person or more while searching for gold by fishing.

Offseason Jacob joined his parents James and Eve Biddle at home in Maryland and used his earnings to help finance repairs to and expand the Biddle Farm. As their only child, he knew one day the farm would be his responsibility, and he fully intended to carry on the family legacy. He unequivocally believed farming was an important and honest occupation.

It took just four seasons for him to surrender his fishing gear for a laptop and classes in different computer programming languages. Eventually he landed with a startup named IndyP Design Studio in Washington State that offered each person that came onboard a stake in the company. Unleashing his creativity, he became part of a diverse team instrumental in designing and building CyberWarriors. It was a video game about an imaginary intergalactic army of laser-wielding soldiers that also employed sonic weaponry to defend the oppressed throughout the galaxy.

So strong was the company's belief in success that no one was astonished when the first release of the copyrighted game garnered a million followers. Almost overnight, IndyP acquired substantial wealth. The game later led to a franchise and that resulted in even greater wealth.

It was at IndyP Design Studio where he met Martha Weaver. She had come onboard for a six-month gig to write content for the studio's website.

He found himself often seated beside her at lunch or a studio-sponsored social outing and enjoyed her company. Her laugh ignited everyone else's laughter, including his. He found her witty, charming, intelligent, and sassy. His parents, diehard fans of 1940 era black and white movies, would describe her as being "spunky" and having "pizzazz."

Soon it was just he and Martha going out, no group. Their shared entertainment excursions included discovering new restaurants, hiking, biking, visiting museums, and attending an occasional movie or concert. Each also valued and guarded their alone time.

After nine months dating, Jacob proposed. Despite the fact they were just ordinary people, both agreed prenups were essential. He had amassed some wealth working for IndyP and she had been awarded a significant settlement from the lawsuit filed after the death of her husband and young son killed in a traffic accident by a drunk driver.

On their lunch hour on a Wednesday, they went to the local courthouse, exchanged vows, and bought lunch from a local taco truck. They didn't share the change in marital status with anyone, not coworkers, not friends, not family. Oddly enough, neither felt compelled to permanently merge households. They were quite comfortable being married but living separately.

Months later, each independently invited their parents to the Seattle area and used a ruse of unexpected apartment repairs to plant them at a five-star hotel. When they all arrived in the lobby to go to dinner, introductions were made, and Jacob and Martha revealed their marriage. All went well, and after spending three days as a family and visiting local sights, the parents went home. Martha's to Alaska, Jacob's to Maryland.

The "we're home safely" call from Martha's parents came first announcing they were in Anchorage and again expressing happiness about their marriage. Jacob's parents didn't call. Shockingly, the Pennsylvania State Police did with the devastating news that his parents were dead. The town car transporting his parents from the airport in Philadelphia to their Maryland home was struck on the freeway during rush hour traffic by a semi-trailer truck whose driver suffered a heart attack. Jacob's parents and the driver of the town car were killed instantly.

Within eight hours, Jacob and Martha were in Principio Furnace arranging for the funeral and interment of his parents next to several generations of Biddles. A month later they moved permanently to Principio. He and Martha took over running Biddle Farms and carved out a new life in the community.

Now, two years later, he was facing another tragedy—the loss of his wife. He sat, head downcast, hands tightly clasped together between his knees, and staring at the floor. The word *why* turned over and over in his mind like a high-powered train running on a looped track. Why was he so conflicted in fostering a child? And then it hit him with the force of a lightning bolt striking a tree.

When Martha told him she was pregnant he was confronted with a mixture of terror and excitement. He contemplated becoming a father and the responsibility it entailed. It was a bit daunting when he created a virtual checklist of the responsibilities he'd share with Martha. Keeping the child safe, healthy, clothed, well fed, and loved were at the top of the list. He had equal responsibility for the well-being of the child, boy or girl. Among other things, he had to serve as a moral compass, as an adjunct teacher. Reflecting on his own childhood, he welcomed becoming a parent.

Then Martha had a miscarriage caused by some bacterial infection the name of which he couldn't even pronounce and again everything changed. He did his best to console her in her misery but failed to seek help for his own pain. In that pain he had forgotten what Martha had not. *Children are a gift from the Lord.*

After making a delivery to the church's food bank, Martha slipped into the church, praying for guidance. When she returned home, she found Jacob sitting on the sofa, hunched over like a man more than twice his age who been beaten down by life's adversities. His hands were intertwined and clasped behind his neck, and though she tried to ignore his posture and forlorn appearance, she couldn't. When he saw her, he looked up, reached out for her right hand, and uttered two words, "Forgive me." She sat down beside him and listened while he carefully and clearly explained why he failed to provide the support she needed when she needed it.

Hours later, Jacob and Martha agreed the Biddle Farm produce market needed to open the next day. Jacob called Miller Newton, Isiah Titter, and Caitlyn Spence to ask if they were able to work the next day, Martha changed the banner on the farm website announcing they were reopening the next day for business. Only Caitlyn, citing the need to help family impacted by the tornado, said no and asked for a few more days off, which Jacob readily agreed to.

Martha and Jacob fed Willy and Dusty and spent time playing with each. After preparing a plate of cheese, crackers, raw vegetables, and apples, they created shopping and to-do lists. One list was identifying items to make the house child-safe. Another was what was needed to provide a secure and child-safe area in the office at the farm. Then there were the vehicles. Both Jacob's truck and Martha's SUV would have to be equipped with child car seats. She had

Jacob search the Internet for current standards and recommendations for the car seats. After reviewing the content and deciding on which product would be appropriate for their respective vehicles, they searched which stores in the area sold the items.

"There are other items, small and large, the child will need," said Martha. "Many of those things can be picked up at one of the second hand stores in the area."

Not knowing what else to say, Jacob muttered, "Okay."

"And then there is the issue of socialization," stated Martha expecting him to give her a quizzical look, which he did.

Her mouth twisted in a partial grin. "The boy will need to spend time with other children. Day care is a good choice but shouldn't be an option during the first three months he's in our care. We—meaning you and me—need to bond with the child and build trust."

"Are you saying you'll need to be at home for the next three months?"

"Oh no, dear. This is hands on. I propose half days, where one of us is home. Do you think we'll need to hire some additional staff to help cover the sale of wreaths, flowers, and trees for the holidays?"

Jacob went pale and Martha held back a smile. "You expect me to spend half days with the child? I know nothing about children. Nothing."

In a calming gesture, she reached out and patted his hand. "You'll learn. I have every confidence in you." Crawling into bed later, Martha covered her mouth to stifle a giggle remembering the look of stark horror on Jacob's face upon learning he, too, would have child watching duty.

WHEN CHIEF COX WALKED INTO THE station less than thirty minutes later, Georgia was just finishing a call, so he just gave a one-handed wave as he went by and entered his office. The call he had taken at the Biddles was from Nick Barrett, providing an update on the medical condition of his granddaughter, Bella. Ken had written down the words Nick used to describe what the doctor said about the ocular injury.

He went to the Internet and searched for information about a corneal abrasion, hyphema, and ended up having more questions than answers.

Frustrated, he called out, "Georgia," and she swiveled around to face him.

"Yes, sir?"

"Nick Barrett called with a summary of his granddaughter's condition. I did a search by using the words he recited, and I don't understand. Do you know of an ophthalmologist who might be able to explain that it means? I don't want to disturb the family again. And, frankly, I don't know if I have the legal right to talk to the surgical oph-thalmologist who examined and treated her at Christiana Hospital."

Understanding the crux of the problem, Georgia said, "Sheriff, Mrs. Barrett faxed a copy of the medical report about Bella to us for inclusion in the complaint they filed."

"Well, that's good news," said the sheriff, and then hopeful asked, "Did you read it?"

"I did. But I don't understand it."

She handed him the file with the medical report and waited while he read it.

"Like you," he told her, closing the file folder. "I don't understand it."

"Would you object, sir, if I called Mrs. Barrett, and asked if she could tell me in plain English, what the outcome, the prognosis, is for her granddaughter?"

"That's a great idea, Georgia," he said enthusiastically, rocking back in his chair. "Make the call. I'm sure Midge Barrett would be happy to share information with us as part of the investigation."

Thirty minutes later, before transcribing the conversation she had recorded with Mrs. Barrett, Georgia summarized it for Chief Cox.

"Mrs. Barrett said her granddaughter, according to the surgeon, suffered 'occular trauma'. That trauma resulted in hyphema. That means there is blood between the anterior chamber of the eye.

The anterior—that's the front part of the eye—is the space between the cornea and the iris."

"Blood?"

"Blood," Georgia confirmed. "The pellet seriously bruised the child's eye. The doctor didn't rule out the possibility Bella could lose vision in the eye. The blood presents an element of danger, and surgery to remove the blood may be required. Bella must see the ophthalmologist weekly to check the collection of blood and eye pressure. And, although difficult for most children, she must limit her activities and wear an eye shield."

"So this is an ongoing problem."

"It appears so."

Chief Cox tapped his desk with the side of a closed fist. "That little girl is just 10. Let's pray she survives the injury and Rose Bender Anderson isn't permitted to put anyone else in danger."

"I'm praying, Chief. So are many others. For both Bella Barrett and for Rose Bender Anderson."

11

Anticipation and Preparation

AN EARLY MORNING GROUP TEXT MESSAGE from Patsy helped set the pace for the day. After preparing Martha's morning coffee and feeding Willy and Dusty, Jacob made himself a cup of tea and accessed the day's to-do list he and Martha had prepared the night before. To the top of the list he added "call the insurance company and find a handyman to install child gates and security door guards." Inspired, he decided to tap his resources and sent out his own group text message asking if anyone could identify a handyman available today and described what he needed done.

Jacob told Martha about the text message and the need to call the insurance company. She opened a cabinet in the built-in desk, pulled out a metal box and then a folder labeled home insurance. Calling the number for the agent listed on the business card attached to the paperwork, she left her name and number, requesting a callback.

Jacob's text query about a handyman drew a response. Clint, Steven, and Earl offered their services. He smiled and expressed his gratitude. *Everyone*, he typed, *is welcome to gather at the Biddle house at 7:30 p.m. to install the necessary protective items in advance of the arrival of our new family member. Refreshments and pizza will be available.* He closed with a happy face meme and in return got thumbs up memes. Earl simply typed okay.

Before they walked out the front door, Jacob asked Martha to print out the images of the gate and security safety guards and to give him the extra door key.

"What's up?" she asked.

Taking the key and printed images from her, he said, "I'm going to ask Earl for more help." He turned on his heel and walked hurriedly out the door, racing toward the Johnson house.

Jackson was barking as Jacob climbed the three steps to the porch. When Harriet opened the door, Jacob's first words were in the form of an apology for knocking at such an early hour. Dismissing it, she said, "You and Martha are family, Jacob. Earl's showering. Tell me what you need?"

He handed her the print outs and asked if Earl could verify the measurements at the top and bottom of the stairs leading to the bedrooms and to the top of the stairs to the basement. "Martha or I can pick up the items at Cornerstone Hardware."

"Or Earl and I could," she suggested.

"That's kind of you, but I can't impose more than I already am, Harriet."

"Dr. Howard said two days, Jacob Biddle," she snapped back in a scolding voice he remembered from his childhood. "Today is the first of those two days and I'm sure Martha has lists in her mind that go beyond what the two of you put together."

He smiled because Harriet nailed it, just like his own mother would have done. Holding up his hands in surrender, he said, "Appreciated."

When Martha and Jacob arrived at the market, Miller and Isiah were waiting outside having an animated conversation. Jacob unlocked the back door to the market, stepped in, and turned on the lights. Martha entered next, followed by the young men, both of whom immediately crossed to the garage doors after Jacob handed them keys to unlock the master lock and then slid open the locking bars at the base of each door.

In two years, Martha learned that farming, including operating a produce market, was rewarding, but it also was hard work. It was sixty minutes before opening, and everyone jumped in to work. So many tasks had to be accomplished in a very short time. Display areas were cleaned and disinfected as appropriate.

Canvas covers and tarps placed over select food products the night before were removed and folded. Produce stacked on shelves in refrigerated sections were pulled, rinsed, and trimmed as necessary, and then put on display. Crates of non-perishable items were unloaded, and existing displays were replenished. Products on display in freezers were rearranged to make items more accessible to customers.

Both Biddles did a final walk through, deftly rearranging produce and other products. The purpose, and they were good at their jobs, was to lead customers to seasonal fruits and vegetables and to draw attention to individual merchandise displays. Biddle Farms not only sold pumpkins and other produce, but had lucrative contracts with other farmers in the area.

Signage, created by Martha and Caitlyn, was added to identify the produce or item and the price. Shopping carts were staged along both sides of the stand. Small paper bags and compostable shopping bags were strategically placed throughout the market for customers to use to carry their chosen produce if they weren't intending to use their own bags. Market floors were swept, cash drawers added to registers, and connectivity to electronic transactions systems to their bank was verified.

Everyone put on the freshly laundered green aprons with Biddle Farms emblazoned across the top panel just before the garage doors were opened. People were already pulling into the parking lot as Jacob and Miller put out the double-sided A-frame signs alerting customers that the market opened at 8:30 a.m. and closed at 6:30 p.m. And Martha knew that with Caitlyn absent, she wasn't going to be able to slip away to shop for goods at the nearest discount department store she needed for Peat's impending arrival. As she had been doing all morning, she silently said *I trust you, Lord, I trust you.*

Martha was pleased to hear Jacob ask Miller and Isiah if they knew anyone interested in working full-time at the market until December twentieth. When asked what kind of work needed to be done, Jacob answered physical labor, explaining only that he and Martha were planning to change their work sched-ules. Both young men exchanged looks sensing that something was up, they just didn't know what that something was.

Just before lunch Martha called the insurance agent again and left another message. Hours later she took advantage of another break in the unexpected throng of customers, many of whom were asking questions about the tornado that hit Principio Furnace days before. She called Bob's Pizza Hut and scheduled a home delivery of pizzas in Principio for 7:30 p.m. She paid by credit card for five extra-large pizzas and added a generous tip for the delivery driver.

At 6 p.m. the parking lot was empty and Jacob called for the shopping carts to be stored away for the night. Then the morning routine was reversed. By 7 p.m. the garage doors were locked and the records of the day's transactions were printed and stored in the onsite safe along with the cash drawers.

"Jacob," said Martha, as she grabbed her purse from a set of keyed lockers installed in the back room and grabbed her car keys, "pizza has been ordered and will be delivered to our home by 7:30. Totally paid for, including the driver's tip. But if you want beer, you'll have to pick it up yourself because I'm going shopping."

"Harriet and Earl picked up the gates and guards."

"I know," she said flashing him a smile. "Harriet texted me. I'll see you at home."

Martha did see Jacob and the crew enlisted to install the child protection devices when she walked in the door at 8:30 p.m. carrying several bags. Earl, Steven, and Clint were in various stages of eating pizza and drinking beer. Smiling broadly, Jacob stepped forward and kissed her. He grabbed the bags she carried and directed her to take a look at their handiwork.

Clasping her hands in utter delight, Martha was thrilled to see every child safety device installed. "It's wonderful, everyone, just wonderful. Thank you very, very much."

"Are there more bags in the car?" Jacob asked her.

Martha replied, "Yes." and added there are also new child carrier seats. He retrieved the bags and Harriet entered behind him.

Upon seeing the car seats, Clint spoke up. "Those can be tricky to install. Can I help?"

Snatching another slice of pizza, Steven piped in, "I can help too," and apologized to his mother for cutting her off.

"That's okay, son," Harriet said, "I just had to see the gates and guards in place. Did you notice, Martha, that we also added safety latches and locks?" She walked over to the cabinet under the kitchen sink and pointed out the new latch.

"Perfect," said Martha.

"There's one in the upstairs bathroom and the half-bath downstairs."

Martha walked over and hugged Harriet saying, "Bless you."

As the child carrier seats were carried back out-side, Earl Johnson pushed away from the dining table and chuckling said, "Well now. I better go supervise the installment."

Harriet shook her head and frowned. "Steven had to install car seats for his children in *our* car. Tell me, Martha, are you going to use a crib for the child?"

"He's a toddler, so it's probably the best choice."

"Do you care if the crib is new or used?" Harriet

believed she already knew the answer, but wanted to hear Martha say it.

"As long as the crib is safe and completely functional, I don't care about color, style, or whether it's new or old."

"The young woman who owns Second Chance in North East is the daughter of my dear friend, Marie Petersen. She also was a friend of Jacob's mother, Eve. I would be happy to call her in the morning and ask her to send pictures of what's currently available in the store."

Martha could only stare at Harriet, who in two years had never purposefully tried to forge a friendship with her, just as she had never wanted a close relationship with Patsy, but for different reasons. She supposed with Harriet part of the reason was generational differences, and she was still trying to reconcile the reasons she rejected a personal relationship with Patsy. Now Martha recognized Harriet for the kind, helpful, caring, and generous woman she truly was, and one without any ulterior motives.

"Harriet, that would be great. With Caitlyn taking extra days off, Jacob and I are in a real pinch at the farm. Today we were swamped. Tomorrow may be a repeat."

"I'll call Marie when I get home, but first, how about showing me what you purchased today."

Smiling, Martha said, "Gladly," and began pulling

out the items she had purchased.

The next day at the farm was exactly as she predicted. Busy. By 10 a.m. Martha stepped into the employee only area and was viewing images of cribs being recycled at Second Chance on Harriet's phone. She and Earl had joined other Biddle Farm shoppers, but with more in mind than picking up some fresh broccoli and Granny Smith apples.

Knowing Jacob would simply tell her to choose whichever crib she liked, Martha pointed to a crib. "Does that look like a model that could be converted to a child's bed to you?"

"It does," said Harriet, and taking back her phone she resized the image. "In fact, other than the color, that's the model Steven and Carol chose for their first child."

"Then that's the one," Maratha said and was glad to check off another item on the top priority list.

"Earl and I will go to North East to check it out."

Taken aback by her generosity, Martha retorted, "You don't have to do that."

Harriet stuck her head out of the back room and scanned the market. "Martha, you can't do it," directing her attention to the number of customers who were packing the market.

Jacob had been surreptitiously watching Harriet and Martha between checking out customers and wishing he could be part of the conversation, whatever it was about.

Earl had been standing in line and watching Jacob's eyes flit between customers in the check-out line and his wife and Harriet. Placing a full bag of Granny Smith apples on the counter next to two crowns of broccoli with stems, Earl told him, "They're talking about cribs."

Martha and Harriet joined their husbands at the counter. Jacob refused to take money from Earl, saying, "We still owe you for the purchases made at Cornerstone."

Martha said, "We're going to owe them even more. They're going to North East and pick up a crib for us."

A surprised Jacob looked from Earl to Harriet and said, "You are?"

Harriet answered, "We are."

Four hours later, Harriet sent an image showing the crib set up in Jacob and Martha's smallest bedroom. Martha was sure the mattress was new and so were the sheets with small, baby blue whales on a white background. In one corner was a small brown teddy bear. Next to the crib was the rocking chair Eve Biddle had used to rock her son to sleep. Now there was a baby blanket draped over one arm of the chair and on its seat was a small needlepoint pillow with the word *Welcome* stitched in bright blue letters.

Martha burst into tears and both Miller and

Isiah, who were closest to her, rushed to her side, asking if she was okay. "I am," Martha told them, "And I'm very happy."

Walking over to Jacob, she showed him the picture, saying "God bless them both. Don't know how they pulled this off, but I'm grateful they did."

Jacob could only say, "Beautiful."

"Besides reimbursing them for the purchases, we're going to do something special for them. Very special," announced Martha.

"I'll ask Steven if he has some suggestions." As Jacob turned to help a customer, his phone rang. Martha stopped in her tracks when she heard him say, "Dr. Howard."

Holding her hands clasped in prayer to her mouth, she listened to the one-sided conversation. "Yes, we'll be home by 7 p.m., Dr. Howard." There was a long pause before he ended the conversation saying, "Yes, we're very ready. We'll see you then."

Martha started doing a happy dance and clicking the heels of her ancient leather loafers together. People laughed and smiled. "Guess that was a good phone call," someone called out and Martha cheerfully answered, "The best."

"Jacob," she started, "There are a few items I must pick up at the store. Can you get along without me for an hour?"

"Sure," Jacob told her, kissing her on the top of

her head.

Shedding her green Biddle Farm apron, she grabbed her purse, jumped in her SUV, and drove into Perryville. As much as she tried to tame her excitement, she couldn't and beamed at everyone she encountered in the store. Like a mad woman running on sheer adrenaline, it took her less than twenty-five minutes to pick up everything she wanted and another 10 to check out. She was back at the market with five minutes to spare.

Jacob saw the glow in Martha's face when she put her apron back on. He told himself that in the last three days he had made the right decisions.

"Did you get everything you wanted?" Jacob asked, and she said nearly.

"I would like a banana, a sweet red apple, a carrot, and a big hug."

He laughed, hugged her, told her he loved her, and collected the produce she requested.

"Anything else?"

"Could you call Caitlyn and tell her we *really* need her to return to work tomorrow?"

Given the circumstances, it was a reasonable request. He made the call.

Precisely at 7 p.m. Jacob and Martha were standing on their porch when Dr. Howard pulled up in front of the house. Jacob ran down the stairs to open the back door of her car and collect the toddler resting in the car seat. As he did, Jill Howard told Martha, who was right behind him, that there was a bag of clothes and other items on the floor.

Martha grabbed the bag, closed the car door, and raced ahead to open the front door. Dr. Howard followed them into the house, taking note of the child safety gates at the both the top and bottom of the staircase when she entered.

Jacob was still holding the boy who seemed fascinated with Jacob's hair because he used his tiny fist in a snatch and grab motion and clutched a good chunk of it. Martha was slowly freeing Jacob's hair from the child's grasp. While she was releasing the child's grip, Dr. Howard sat down at the dining table and opened a file she pulled from her purse.

"You might want to let the boy sit there," pointing to the play pen with the mesh sides that Martha had purchased hours before, "because there are forms you and Martha need to sign."

"Let me give you assurances that the pneumonia is gone. He's been fed," she said, "His nurse's say he has a healthy appetite and likes his sippy cup. It's in the bag you picked up from the back seat."

Martha dug into the bag and pulled out sippy cup. She also pulled out an orange-colored fuzzy monkey that looked like it had seen better days.

Seeing the scrawny monkey in Martha's hand, Dr. Howard smiled and said, "I'm told he really likes the monkey. It just magically appeared. Don't know if the monkey is washable. I didn't attempt to wash it, but I can tell you all the clothes in the bag were laundered," then adding, "by me."

Martha handed the boy the monkey and was surprised to see him smile, showing all his primary teeth. She also heard him emit a guttural sound when he took the stuffed animal. The sound grew louder, more excited, and he was pumping his arms up and down when he saw Willy and Dusty sitting just outside the play pen and staring back at him. The attention of all three adults automatically shifted to the scene with both cats turning and sending a "what have you done" look to Jacob and Martha. Everyone laughed.

They signed the paperwork and Dr. Howard said they would be sent a copy of it. "Any questions?" she asked as she inserted the paperwork in the file and tucked it back in her purse.

"In the interest the child, who I fully intend to call Peat, spelled with an 'a', how do we refer to ourselves?"

It took Dr. Howard a moment to process Martha's question. "Are you asking what the child should call you and Jacob?"

"Yes," answered Martha, crossing her arms.

"Are we aunt and uncle?" Jacob asked.

"Are you comfortable using those definitions?"

Jacob and Martha exchanged glances.

"I haven't discussed this with Jacob, Doctor, but Peat does have a mother and a father. They may have abandoned him, and they may have an excellent reason for doing so, all of which I pray to God was done to protect the boy. But honestly, I'm uncomfortable breaching that familial connection unless they come forward and make statements that reveal otherwise."

"Jacob, do you agree with your Martha?"

Without hesitation, he said, "I do. It sounds reasonable."

"So, you don't want to be referred to as Mom and Dad?" Dr. Howard stated. "Understandable." Then she picked up her purse and said, "Peat seems to be nodding off, so I'll say goodnight. Call me if you have any questions. I'll check in with you in a few days."

They both walked her to the door, and Jacob walked her to her car.

Before reentering the house, Jacob bent down and picked up the white envelope lying on the porch to the right of the door.

"Is he sleeping?" Jacob asked.

"He is," she went over to the dining table and started examining the clothes from the bag. "Tomorrow Peat and I will go shopping."

Martha saw Jacob place the envelope on the table. "What's in the envelope?"

"Don't know. It's probably a card from Harriet or

Patsy."

"Let's see," Martha said as she opened the unsealed envelope and pulled out a card.

Jacob saw the color drain from her face as she held up the card she had pulled from the envelope. It wasn't a card, but a photograph. It was a photograph of a child's navel with a birthmark that looked like a finely etched pumpkin tendril.

Shocked, Jacob said, "Dear Lord."

Clutching her chest, Martha asked, "What's written on the back of the photo, Jacob?"

"Thank you. Be kind and love him."

"What do we do now, Jacob?"

His answer was unexpected, "We lock the doors, put Peat to bed, and have a glass of cold apple cider. In the morning, we'll call Chief Cox."

12

Moving Forward

KEN COX WAS THIRD GENERATION MILITARY and as such had grown accustomed to leading a regimented, orderly life. Now living the life of a civilian, he tried his best to maintain a certain level of structure professionally. For him it meant honoring his parents and grandparents by leading and living by example following the moral code they taught him and the ethics they instilled in him.

As sheriff he detested putting his personal needs before those of his officers. It was his policy to schedule any personal appointments, especially medical-related, on his day off. Ken didn't like having to schedule an early morning medical appointment on a workday, but his wife, Alison, had insisted because he had missed two previous appointments. Alison's concerns were warranted. Having a prosthetic and failing to meet with a doctor routinely was not a good thing.

When he walked into the station at 8:30 a.m., he was making every effort to shake off his bad temper. He said hello to Officer Georgia Straw and took the telephone message she held out, noting a call from Jacob Biddle came in at 7 a.m. He wasn't ready to return the call.

Ken grabbed a cup of coffee and the daily activity logs. In his office, he dropped down into the swivel banker's chair and began reading the activities entered in the log for the previous night.

Three incidents were recorded by Charles Edmondson officer on duty. One involved the discovery of five young people, all underage, drinking hard liquor and smoking pot in a park behind the local high school. A second entry was a noise complaint, and the third was an alarm at a local office building accidentally tripped by new janitorial staff.

The parents of two females and three males found partying were called to collect them at the scene, even though all lived within walking distance. In the presence of their parents, each juvenile was given a verbal warning and cautioned that any future abuses, however minor, would be referred to the city attorney for possible prosecutorial action.

The third entry in the log really drew Ken's attention. It was recorded as a noise complaint against a tenant in an apartment that ended up being investigated as a domestic violence incident. Ken recognized the name of the man in the complaint as a repeat offender. Because there was an outstanding warrant for the man's arrest, the state troopers were called and transported him to the barracks on Route 40.

When Chief Cox returned Jacob Biddle's phone call, he was only mildly surprised to learn that a message related to the abandoned boy was hand-delivered to the Biddle's front door. He was more surprised to learn it was dropped just feet away from where the Biddles and Dr. Jill Howard were gathered in the living room as they accepted the child into foster care. Given the fact the photograph left on the doorstep showed the boy's unique birthmark, it was indisputable evidence that the child was known by the messenger.

Chief Cox, about to say, "Mr. Biddle," caught himself and instead said, "Jacob. I urge you, for your safety and peace of mind, to install a camera system that videotapes activity outside your house and at the farm."

"I plan to do exactly that," answered Jacob, who had already scheduled an appointment with a security surveillance firm in the area.

"Whoever these people are Jacob," warned the Chief, "they'll be back."

Alarmed by his words, Jacob said, "You don't think whoever they are would hurt the child or Martha, do you?"

Deciding to forego the usual platitudes, the Chief Cox got straight to the point.

"These are people who deliberately left a child in your pumpkin patch. At best, their intention could have been to find a safe haven for the child. At worse, their intention could have been to place the child in an environment that they knew they could potentially extort money from the caregivers. These people could be sophisticated scam artists, who researched you and your wife and followed you at every opportunity, learning your routines and habits."

The suggestion stunned Jacob. "I never thought of that," he said slowly.

"Just speculation, Jacob, but caution is paramount. And I will be talking with Dr. Howard to see if she saw anyone or anything."

"I assume you'll alert me if she did." The sheriff ended the conversation with, "You assume right."

Jacob stood like a statue, lost in his own world, eyes downcast, his mobile phone clasped in his right hand. Caitlyn had been repeatedly calling out his name trying to get Jacob's attention and failed.

Finally, she boldly placed herself in front of him saying in a louder voice, "Jacob, there's a man here to see you," she said, and handed Jacob the business card the man had passed to her.

Looking up, Jacob squeezed out a smile, said, "Thank you, Caitlyn," and walked out and introduced himself to the man.

There was a lull in customers, so Miller and Isiah walked over to Caitlyn.

"So now do you agree that he's acting weird?" Miller asked her.

"Yeah."

"Did you notice the car seat in the back seat of his truck?" asked Isiah.

"I did," said Caitlyn, who was watching Jacob and the unknown man talking outside the market. "It's a rear-facing car seat used for infants and toddlers." Both threw her a 'how do you know that look' so she added, "My cousin, Abby, had a baby last year. She has the same car seat."

"Jacob asked us to identify potential workers and asked you to return to work, Caitlyn. So where's Martha, huh?" Miller asked. Caitlyn could only shrug her shoulders in response.

After feeding, bathing, and dressing Peat, Martha called Harriet and Earl and invited them to dinner Saturday night. Then she loaded Peat in her SUV, and headed to North East to do some shopping. As adorable as she found his helmet of corkscrew curls, she actually wanted to create a distance between her and Jacob and the picture of the abandoned child in the paper. She popped into Cuts for Tots.

A young woman with pink hair standing inside the door said, "Welcome to Cuts for Tots." Then she clamped her hands together when she saw Peat, and proclaimed, "Oh my goodness, what a luscious head of hair!"

"Yes, it is," responded Martha as she watched the young woman who introduced herself as Darcy place a booster seat on a regular salon chair.

"If you prefer, the child can sit in the airplane or the car station."

Martha ran her free hand over Peat's head, saying, "I think he might like the airplane."

Once positioned in the child-size plane and a cape covered with colorful balloons draped over his shoulders, Darcy asked, "Who is this little guy?"

"Peat."

"How short do you want Peat's hair?"

"Half inch."

Darcy's eyebrows lifted in surprise. "Half inch it is."

Thirty minutes later, the floor was covered in black curls, and Peat looked like a different child.

"You're a good boy, Peat," Darcy told the boy who now was twisting and turning the wheel to the airplane.

"Yes, he is," said a smiling Martha. "Good job, Darcy."

"Does he talk?"

It was a question Martha had been asking herself all morning. She responded with, "Yes" and was shocked when the boy said in a small voice something that sounded like 'oose'.

"Let me pay Darcy, Peat, and then we'll go get some juice."

Martha made a quick stop at a roadside market for apple juice poured some into the sippy cup she had stuffed in a large cloth tote and handed it to the boy. She also pulled out a small dish and was delighted when Peat took the juice and reached into the dish for a baby carrot.

After the market, Martha made a beeline for Second Chance. She introduced herself as a friend of Harriet and Earl Johnson.

"You must be Martha, Jacob's wife," said a petite, dark-haired woman who extended her hand. "I'm Whitney Petersen Carson." Martha judged the woman to be in her late thirties and extended her hand.

"And this," announced Martha, as she shifted the child from one hip to the other, "is Peat."

"The recipient of the crib?"

"Yes, now I'm looking for a stroller and some clothing."

"I can help you with a stroller but not clothing." She guided Martha over to a section that had a range of strollers.

The one jogging stroller caught her eye. "This I like," she said as she dropped Peat into the seat.

Looking at the size of the child, Whitney said truthfully, "I'm glad, it's a great stroller. But he'll likely grow out of it by summer."

"You're probably right," agreed Martha. "He'll probably need a Radio Flyer for transportation by then."

Whitney threw back her head and laughed. Startled by the outburst, Peat started to cry. Martha picked him up, gently rubbed his back, and in a low, soft, soothing voice uttered comforting words.

"I'm so-o-o sorry," Whitney whispered. "I didn't mean to frighten the child."

"He's fine."

"You're a good mom. You calmed him down instantly," Whitney said.

Martha corrected her, "Not mom, aunt."

"Oh. No matter. You certainly have a knack for settling the boy. Do you want the stroller?"

"I do. But you don't recycle clothing?"

"No, I don't. And I don't know anyone in the area who does."

Martha plopped Peat down on the counter and pulled out her credit card.

"Where are you parked?" Whitney asked.

"Within walking distance."

Whitney pushed the stroller out the door and onto the sidewalk. Martha lowered Peat in the stroller, said "Thank you very much," and made her way to the car.

Martha stopped on the way home to buy Peat more clothes and a pair of slipper booties. She was stunned when he was fitted with a bootie for a four-year-old. Martha suspected the child had probably never worn a slipper or a shoe of any kind. By the time she fed him and laid him down for a nap, he had pulled off the slippers and his socks.

It wasn't until her office was closing for lunch, that Dr. Jill Howard was handed a message that Sheriff Cox had telephoned. After the meeting at the Biddle house with Martha and Jacob and their neighbors, she simply couldn't think why Ken was calling.

She went to the small kitchen in the clinic and retrieved her lunch bag. Back at her desk, she took several bites out of her turkey sandwich before returning Ken's call.

He answered the call himself. "It's Jill Howard."

"Thank you for returning my call, Dr. Howard."

"How can I help you?"

"Jacob Biddle called me this morning."

"Is everything okay?"

"Yes and no," he answered cryptically. "You delivered the abandoned child into his and his wife's care last night?"

Frowning, Jill wondered what was behind his question. "I did. Legally. Why are you interested?"

"Because a message was left for the Biddles."

Her senses now heightened, Jill asked, "What

kind of message?"

Detecting an element of strain in her voice, he said, "A non-threatening message. But a clear message that the Biddles and the child are being watched."

"What was the message?"

"A photograph."

"Of the boy?"

"No, his birthmark."

"Oh, dear. A very clear message."

"Exactly. On the back of the photograph were the words 'Thank you, be kind, love him.'"

"Non-threatening," Jill said, echoing his word. "So the message was delivered this morning?"

"No. It was delivered to the Biddle house last night when you were there."

Her mind was spinning, "What?"

"The picture was in a white envelope dropped on the porch in front of the door. Jacob said it wasn't there when you entered the house, and he didn't notice it until after he walked you outside and returned to the house."

He heard her sigh. Finally she said, "How could three adults, within a foot of the front door, miss someone on the Biddle porch?"

"Perhaps you saw something, but what you saw didn't raise any red flags at the time," the chief suggested.

The silence lasted so long that he said, "Dr. Howard, are you still there?"

Jill felt a tug at her memory because of his words. Finally she said, "I am thinking."

"You think you saw something." It wasn't a question, but a statement.

Hesitating, she said, "I'm not sure. There was a moment . . . I can't . . ."

He waited, not speaking, distracted by a police report that had just landed on his desk. He gave Dr. Howard time to tap into her memory without interruption from him.

Her sharp exclamation of "Red!" jolted him.

Dropping the report, he said, "Red?"

"Yes, red," she repeated, and he heard a note of excitement in her voice. "There were red tail lights in front of me."

"You saw the tail lights of a vehicle in front of you when you left the Biddles?"

"Yes."

"Can you describe the vehicle?"

"No, but I can tell you it was a dark color, and I think much smaller and older than my vehicle." Ken knew Jill Howard drove a silver Ford Explorer.

"Did you notice anything else about the vehicle? Was it a Maryland license plate?"

"I'm sure I would have noticed if it wasn't a Maryland license plate."

Slightly disappointed, he said, "If you should remember anything at all, please call me."

"Oh, there was one strange thing."

"What was that?"

"Both of us were driving toward Perryville, but all of a sudden, I could no longer see their tail lights. I didn't see them pull off the road into the Biddle Market, so I don't know where they went."

"That's very curious, Doctor. When you were behind the car, were you close enough that your headlights were illuminating their interior? If so, was there a passenger?"

Thinking back, Jill said, "You know. . .I believe there was."

"Thank you, Doctor."

"I don't think I gave you any useful information, Chief Cox."

"Every little bit helps."

He had hoped there would be more, much more, but there wasn't. But Ken thought he knew where the car might have pulled off. It actually was a spot past the Biddle Market that the department used to catch speeders.

13

Unexpected Rescue

R ETIREMENT HAD BEEN ON HER MIND for days and just that morning she had decided that it was time to quit teaching. She had run the numbers and financially could do it. More importantly, she could emotionally do it. There were many nights that cruising to some exotic island in the Caribbean filled her dreams. She might be five years from legal retirement, but at 60 she was ready for new adventures in her life that didn't include teaching toddlers.

For now, she had settled for a walk to a nearby park and decided to sit on the bench with the cast iron plaque pinned that read "Dedicated to Ethel Mae Craig, who loved this park." She pulled out a paperback book from her canvas tote she'd been looking forward to reading for months.

Before she turned to the first page, her eyes were drawn to the bright red Cardinal that had landed in a large pine tree that stood in front of the bench, and then to a young girl and an older man who crossed in her line of sight. As she watched their encounter unfold, the phrase "see something, say something" relentlessly tracked like the steady click of a metronome in her head. Cassie's internal alarm bell didn't signal high danger until the man reached out and appeared to tightly grab the young woman's upper arm, forcing her to yell out and causing her to turn and reveal an infant child wrapped under her coat. The battered wheeled suitcase the girl had been pulling behind her fell to the ground.

Then seemingly out of nowhere an older woman ran forward to the man and girl and Cassie held her breath thinking the woman was coming to offer assistance to the girl being assaulted. When the woman yanked the girl's other arm, Cassie's hope turned to vapor. The young girl clearly wasn't a match physically for the man or the woman and neither would Cassie be if she was foolish and tried to rush forward to help.

Wanting to draw the attention and assistance of other people in the park, Cassie screamed out several times at the top of her lungs, "Nooooo! Help, they're trying to kidnap a girl and her child. Help!bHelp!"

Who was yelling help? In a lucid moment, she realized it was herself, but someone else was calling her name.

"Cassie?" There it was again. "It's Jessica. Cassie, are you okay?" And then she heard the knocking, followed again by someone asking loudly. "Cassie, are you okay?" Was she okay she asked herself? And in that instant, she realized she had been dreaming, but all of it had been real.

Cassie sat up, brushed her hair away from her eyes and glanced at the clock on her nightstand. It was midnight. "I'm good. Go back to sleep. Had a nightmare." Except it wasn't a nightmare. It was an embedded memory. And her cousin Jeb's wife, Jessica, was now part of that memory. She supposed it wasn't uncommon for many families to have a Jessica in their midst—a "fixer" who could have easily been a nurse but wasn't. She, gratefully, was a natural caregiver. Whenever someone in the family needed help, Jessica was there.

She fell back into her pillow and tapped into the still fresh memory. She recalled how she screamed out for help and then opened her cell phone and dialed 911. Her heart pumping rapidly and ringing in her ear, as calmly and quickly as she was able, Cassie gave the 911 operator her location and briefly described the assault she witnessed, emphasizing the presence of an infant. About the time she heard the police sirens, she saw some of the men playing football at the other end of the park charge toward the scene. Cassie was right behind them, screaming at the man and the woman to let the girl go, and telling the girl to run toward her because the police were on their way.

The older man grabbed the girl again, trying to pull her away, but one of the men with the moves of a quarterback who had raced to help bellowed, "Let her go!" Though the senior man tried to maintain his hold, he couldn't as the younger, and clearly stronger, man pried his hand from his hold on the girl's upper arm. Cassie raced forward, wrapped her arms around the shaking and sobbing girl's shoulders, and gently pulled her away from the scene.

"My child," cried the girl, her body crumbling with convulsive sobs, "They … want … my … child."

Cassie told her softly, "You and your child are now safe," and she silently prayed it was true. When she looked back the man was being held between two younger men and the woman was gone.

When approached by a policeman, Cassie, her arm still wrapped around the shoulder of the young girl, answered "Yes" when asked if she was the one who called 911.

As she and the girl were being escorted to a police car, Cassie asked, "Can someone please pick up the girl's suitcase?" as they were escorted toward a police car.

"Did you catch the older woman?" Cassie asked the police officer as she slid into the back seat of the patrol car, momentarily surprised about how uncomfortable it was, but then realized it was designed to be.

The officer, who still carried the shine of a new recruit, stopped in his tracks. "What older woman?"

"She grabbed the girl minutes before a young man pulled the older man away. I saw her run toward the cars along the north side of the park when the police sirens got louder."

"Thank you. I'll inform the officer in charge." He stepped aside and spoke into the radio clipped to his shirt and then closed the door and told the driver to go. "Wait," Cassie called out. "I need to collect my tote and book near the bench." Without waiting for a response, she opened the door, dashed over to the bench and collected her possessions, then ran and crawled back into the car.

In a very short time they were in the parking lot reserved for police cars behind the multistory brick building downtown in the heart of Lancaster. The police officer grabbed the suitcase from the front seat, helped the young girl and her infant out of the car, and then escorted them and Cassie inside the home of the city's Bureau of Police originally established in 1865. Once in the lobby, Cassie asked that the mother and child be sequestered in a private room. The child was now crying, possibly hungry, and perhaps in need of a diaper change.

Once in a small room, the mother opened the suit-case and pulled out a dry diaper, there was no question the child was male. Cassie was shocked to see an abundance of dark curls framing a small pale face with stunningly bright blue eyes. His mother's eyes.

"He's beautiful. What's his name?" asked Cassie.

"Theo," she said as she rocked the child slowly. "It means gift of God. At least that what's the Internet says. Well, Google. It's Greek."

"I'm Cassie."

"And I'm Nora. Thanks for your help. Don't know what I would have done without it."

"Nora, I'm glad you and your son are safe. Was the man really trying to take your son?"

"Yes. So was his wife."

Shocked, Cassie said, "The woman who grabbed your arm is his wife?"

Nora nodded yes, and muttered, "She's very mean and both are really rotten people!"

"Do you have family nearby that can help you?"

Watching the girl's lower lip quiver, Cassie reached out and touched Nora's hand, saying, "No worries, I have a small duplex on Water Street. You and Theo can stay with me until the police finish their investigation, and you can decide what your next step will be."

"But you don't know me," protested Nora, flabbergasted by the unexpected offer from a woman who was a stranger.

Before Cassie could respond, there was a tap on the door and a tall, muscular policeman entered wearing a short-sleeve dark green T-shirt with a badge hanging from a lanyard around his neck. The man introduced himself as Detective Harry Waite, handing both women a business card that showed he was part of the Special Investigative Unit.

Cassie stood and said, "I'm Cassie. Cassie Cooper, the person who called 911. Can we . . ." and was cut off by the detective, saying, "Jeb Cooper's second cousin who he calls CC?" Cassie should have been surprised but wasn't. It was, after all, a small community.

"Well, Detective, you're well informed."

"He heard your name called over the police band."

Keeping her eyes on Nora, who nestled her son in her arms, Cassie saw the woman visibly relax hearing the exchange between her and the detective. "I just offered Nora and her son, Theo, a refuge as the investigation unfolds. I'd be grateful for several things. The first is a request that my involvement is kept confidential. The public doesn't need to know. I'll leave you my address and phone number."

She looked back at Nora and said, "It'll be okay" but before she could close the door behind her, the detective stepped in. Cassie drew back and stared at the detective. He didn't blink under her undisguised scrutiny. She guessed the man was still in his forties. It took her a bit of time to pull a name out of her memory bank and then said, "I'm guessing Amanda inherited her curly red hair from your wife, but she definitely shares facial features with you."

"And you were Amanda's first grade teacher. I believe it was the poem, *The Little Turtle*, that you often recited, inspired her to adopt turtles as pets."

He smiled, which softened the sharp angles of his face. "I am. She's in fifth grade now and still has curly red hair. And because of you, still has a passion for turtles. At last count, she has three."

Smiling Cassie said, "Ah. Can we chat privately in the hallway for a minute?"

"Absolutely," he responded. "Other requests?"

"Today can you ask Nora general information, and then come to my place tomorrow to conduct an in-depth interview?"

"I'll be interviewing both you and Nora."

Cassie didn't expect that statement. "Would 9:30 a.m. work?"

"It will."

"And could I ask for a patrol car . . ."

"Already arranged."

"Thank you."

"Thank Jeb."

"Thank me for what?" came a deep baritone voice behind her.

She spun around to see her cousin Jeb, six years her junior walking down the hall toward her.

"C'mon, CC. You know Coopers always take care of Coopers."

Cassie smiled and walked into Jeb's extended arms. She pulled away and said, "And you told Jessica about today's events, didn't you?"

"You know I never lie to my wife."

She chuckled. "Uh, huh," noticing a slight thickening in his waistline. "Except for the daily stops at La Dolce Vita bakery?"

Jeb responded with "Shhh," and she caught Detective Waite standing in the background grinning.

It was Jeb who drove her, Nora, and Theo to her home. Within thirty minutes of their arrival Jessica swooped in with a bassinette that Cassie recognized. Cassie had gifted it to Jessica and Jeb's third daughter, Harriet, who gave birth to their fourth grandchild three years ago. She also came with bags of her famous homemade chicken noodle soup, some sandwiches from the neighborhood sub shop, jars of organic baby food, and some clothes for Theo and his mother.

Cassie had deposited Theo and Nora in the guest room shortly after they had entered and now called them out for introductions. Jessica cooed over Theo and asked Nora if it was okay if she fed him some organic carrots and sliced bananas. When Nora said it was, Jessica grabbed the bassinette, draped a beach towel over it, and then propped up Theo inside it using towels and hung a big bib around his neck.

Everyone laughed when Jessica, who had pulled a baby spoon from a pocket on the apron she wore, scooped some cooked carrot from the jar, and Theo grabbed her hand and pulled it toward himself.

By the time everyone had grabbed some breakfast, Detective Waite was knocking on the door. Cassie welcomed him in. He greeted everyone, including Jessica, who he wasn't surprised to see holding Theo. Then he announced that the man and the woman who had assaulted Nora the day before were arrested earlier that morning.

"I still need to interview Miss Cooper and Miss Jones," he said.

"If you want privacy, Detective Waite, the other side of my duplex is empty," Cassie said.

Nora piped in, "I'm fine answering questions with everyone present."

Clearly skeptical, the detective asked, "You're sure?" When she said yes, he pulled a notebook and pen from a nylon style briefcase. He started by interviewing Cassie. It was short. The interview with Nora wasn't. He asked in-depth questions about her background and an hour later, Cassie knew a lot more about Nora, including the name of Theo's now deceased father—Trey Mitchell. And Nora's explanation of the events surrounding his death at 25 wove a story that led to an explanation of what happened in the park.

"Trey and I shared a love of agriculture, particularly farming. In the last four years, he developed a major interest in hydroponics. We were heading toward Maryland when Trey decided he wanted to talk with Amish farmers and ask if they knew about the process and what they thought about it."

The detective said, "So, you traveled to Lancaster County, well-known home to the Amish."

"We did. It became clear pretty soon that traveling the back roads was a problem because of nutty, dangerous drivers. Most had no respect for sharing a country road with people in a horse and buggy for transportation."

"You were driving Route 896?" asked Detective Waite.

Nora didn't answer him. She paused, her thin eyebrows drawn together, and then said, "Trey told me to grab the cell phone, to climb into the back seat, buckle in, and sit next to Theo."

She paused and took a sip of water before continuing. "Horns were blaring and people hanging out car windows shouting for us to move, but we couldn't. There was nowhere to go. Nowhere," her voice rose sharply with each word she with each word she spoke.

"Trey told me to call 911 and I did. I put the phone on speaker mode. He told the operator we were heading southbound toward Maryland on

Route 896 but couldn't give any other markers. A second later the car behind us deliberately hit our car. Then they slammed our car a second time hard enough to pitch us forward and Trey I guess instinctively braked. I screamed and reached out to make sure Theo was okay."

In the silence that ensued, Cassie realized Nora was reliving the event. "It was a nightmare," she declared. "The car that deliberately hit us triggered a chain event where the cars behind it hit the one in front of them. You get the picture."

Detective Waite spoke up, "I remember the pictures in the paper. It was quite a pileup."

"I remember them too," said Cassie. "The photos were . . . disturbing."

"What they didn't show was really disturbing," said Nora. Her expression was grim. "After the second hit our car was sitting at an angle in the road. Three young men in the car that hit us jumped out and were dragging Trey out of our car and punching him. They threw him to the ground and started kicking him. He couldn't fight back. They were muscular; he wasn't. I kept pleading for help, while trying to protect and calm Theo who was wailing."

"Others must have been calling for help because the police finally arrived. Weapons drawn, they shut down the thugs beating Trey. Other cops appeared and pulled the men off him."

"Trey was in bad shape and was transported by ambulance to the nearest hospital. One of the officers helped me pull out our personal belongings and suitcases from the vehicle and retrieve records we kept in the glove compartment. He drove me and Theo to the hospital, and we were led to an area near the intensive care unit and escorted to some room provided with a nurse volunteer to help with Theo."

"Two days later Trey died. They hit him and beat him so badly that they caused a brain bleed that the doctors couldn't stop. All three were charged with his death and the cause of all the accidents. And it was the parents of one of the young men responsible for Trey's death who tried to abduct me and Theo."

"They tracked me down to a location that attorney John Sterbick and his associate Marlene Robinson arranged for me and Theo to stay."

Detective Waite said, "Don't know the man personally, but the firm of John Sterbick is well known in the community and well respected. He's known for winning civil cases. And he helped a good family friend through a battle—and scored a win—against the mighty IRS."

"Good to know," said Nora, "because I'm relying on him to help me navigate through all the legal issues that I may encounter."

Neither Detective Waite nor Cassie said a word.

14

Revelations and Justice

After Nora spoke, the ensuing silence was pierced by a child's giggling and Jessica's "oh my goodness." All three dashed into the other room. Jessica was tickling Theo's belly and exposing a very distinct birthmark on his belly. He was pumping his little legs in excitement as Jessica lightly used the tip of her index finger to draw circles around his belly button. The effervescence of his giggles drew laughter from the adults.

"I've never seen a birthmark quite like his," announced Jessica. "At first, I thought it was a tattoo, and I confess to experiencing a spike of outrage. It looks like the tendril you find on the stem of a pumpkin. Quite beautiful."

"Trey had the same birthmark," Nora said, and then shook her head and added, "Not exactly the same, but similar."

"Seriously?" asked a frowning Cassie. "I've never

heard about hereditary birthmarks." Glancing back at Theo's bellybutton, she said, "It's unusual and most certainly beautiful."

Detective Waite's phone rang. He answered telling the caller that he'd be there shortly. "Apologies ladies, I have to go but I do have a few more questions for you, Nora. I'll call you to arrange another time to meet."

Glancing back at the exposed birthmark, he stated, "That birthmark is remarkable." He grabbed his notebook and pen and slipped them into his briefcase before turning and leaving.

About fifteen minutes after the detective left, Cassie told Nora she was going for a walk and told her to yell out for the police officer posted outside the duplex if she had a problem.

Nora responded by telling Cassie and Jessica, "Enjoy your walk. Theo and I will be fine."

To Nora, Jessica simply said, "My daughter is expecting me to join her at her doctor's appointment. There's a jar of freshly smashed sweet potatoes, and another of cooked carrots, and there's a small bag of cheese for Theo in the fridge. And there's some apple juice. Let me know if you need me to look after Theo tomorrow." Then she grabbed her purse, pulled out her car keys, and with a smile turned and walked out the door.

Cassie paused to say hello to the on-duty officer,

asked if she needed water or food, and when she declined both, she advised her that she was going for a walk. Two blocks away Cassie pulled out her phone and called Jessica.

When she answered, Cassie asked if she could meet her at Big Jake's Place or was she really meeting her daughter at the doctor's office?

"No. Are you at Big Jake's?"

"Ten minutes away. I'll be sitting outside."

"On my way."

Within fifteen minutes, Jessica sat down across from her and asked, "What are you drinking?"

"A shandy? Well, Ann's version of one."

"That's the drink your Australian friend introduced you to?"

"Yes. A ginger ale and a splash of beer. It's refreshing."

"I'll try one."

When Penny the barmaid stepped out to take Jessica's order, Jessica simply said that she'd have the same as Cassie.

Once she sipped the drink, Jessica declared with a note of surprise, "Refreshing is a good description. Why have I never tried this before?"

Bluntly Cassie said, "You rejected the idea of mixing a soda with a beer."

"Stupid me."

Cassie laughed, "Exactly!"

"Jessica, what did you think about Nora's story today?"

"Aside from her being very animated, she provided details never revealed in the news article."

"Bet the police reported it but the paper declined to include details in the news article."

"I never read anything about the men being drunk. Wonder what their blood alcohol levels were."

"Surely they exceeded the .08 percent."

"Bet you're right. Still, no excuse. No one should ever be drinking and getting behind the wheel of a car. We've all driven that road and know to drive slowly and carefully to respect the Amish and others."

"Her anger is justified. Those angry young men killed her husband."

"I'm sure there's more to come. Although the exposure of Theo's birthmark was certainly astonishing."

"It was, wasn't it!"

"After you and Detective Waite left, she said a few things."

"Spill."

"She told me two of her and Trey's suitcases were still in the hospital locked in the office of the social worker who provided comfort to her and Theo and she needed to retrieve them."

"You of course offered to take her to the hospital?"

"I did."

"And she also said she needed to talk with John Sterbick, the lawyer, about several matters, without elaborating about what."

"But the very first thing she announced was that she needed to know where her husband's body is and that she needed to make arrangements to have him cremated so she could have his ashes buried with his grandparents."

"Cremated?"

"Yes. She said her husband wanted his ashes interred in the grave of his grandparents in New Jersey after his parents died. They died of COVID-19."

"New Jersey? Didn't she tell you she didn't have family?"

Cassie frowned and said, "She did and when I reminded her of that she stated, 'I don't, Trey did.' Then she proceeded to tell me that she was raised in the foster care system in Oklahoma and definitely doesn't have family."

"Oh my," exclaimed Jessica.

"She didn't stop there."

"No?"

"No," and rolling her eyes skyward, Cassie said, "C'mon, you and I, particularly you, have observed her lack of interest in her son." Jessica nodded. "She told me she hasn't a single maternal instinct in her body.

Trey, she said, was both father *and* mother and that she intended to choose who will raise Theo."

Shocked, Jessica said sharply, "What the heck does that mean?"

"I don't know, and frankly, her remark scares me."

"Of course it does. What are you going to do?"

Taken aback, Cassie responded with, "What can I do?"

"Tell Jeb."

Cassie flashed Jessica a drop-dead look before saying, "Repeating what the girl said when there's no associative action? I don't think so. Many people talk of doing things, and then do nothing."

"And do you think she'll do nothing?"

Cassie pursed her lips, then sighed and said, "I don't know. But I've decided that I have no right to judge her. In fact, since she and Theo entered my life, I've had to revisit past events, both joyful and sad, in my life and came to a single conclusion."

"What conclusion?"

Taking another sip of the shandy, she said, "We hide in our memories."

JESSICA GOT THE CALL ASKING IF she could watch Theo the following week. It was the same week that the criminal trial was set to begin for the three young men who were directly responsible for the tragic death of Trey Williams. In addition to the criminal case, John Sterbick filed multiple civil lawsuits against the men in the criminal case as well as one against the parents who tried to abduct Nora and Theo.

In the criminal cases, it took only three days for the prosecutor to present evidence of the heinous acts they committed. It ended in a charge of DUI felony for each defendant and justifiably in a ruling of seven years imprisonment for each.

A penalty of one year of jail was given to the parents who tried to snatch Nora and Theo in the park. Sterbick & Associates won each civil lawsuit filed against the parents and the criminal defendants. It took longer for the civil cases to be processed. Nora ended with sizable financial awards by juries who objected to people who robbed a young woman of a husband and a young son of his father.

Nora never revealed the exact sum of money she'd receive. Cassie didn't ask.

CASSIE WAS HOLDING HER ANGER IN check as best she could, but over the last few days that effort grew increasingly more difficult. As a teacher of little ones she was quite accustomed to practicing kindness and restraint. The current situation, however, was extraordinarily challenging.

She had offered to take Nora and Theo to New Jersey to visit the grave of her husband's grandparents where Trey's ashes had been interred months before. The plan was that afterward mother and child would travel via train to New York and reconnect with some of Nora's friends there.

On the day of departure, Jessica arrived to say good-bye to Nora and to Theo, with whom she had grown very attached. Theo clutched his monkey and Jessica cried as he was placed in the car seat in the back seat of Cassie's old car. A single suitcase containing Nora's essentials was placed next to Theo. So was an overnight case for Cassie. Jessica stood on the sidewalk as Cassie pulled away, waving good-bye as she did.

As they traveled out of Lancaster, Nora suddenly expressed a desire to visit the location where she and Trey were headed to months before.

"Where were you going?" asked Cassie.

"Biddle Farm near Principio Furnace," said Nora.

"Never been there," answered Cassie flatly and really had absolutely no desire to go there now.

Nora said enthusiastically, "Biddle Farm and its produce market was a happy place for me and Trey. It's closer to Principio Furnace, but let's go through Perryville. Connect to Highway 40, head toward Perryville."

Forcing a smile, Cassie said, "Fine by me. Next stop, Perryville," as she shifted into drive and headed toward Maryland.

SEVERAL DAYS LATER, CASSIE WAS STILL outraged about Nora's actions when they arrived at the Biddle Farm Market stand located off Old Route 7 in Maryland. Despite being closed, Nora insisted on parking behind a grove of trees fronted by the remnants of a pumpkin patch.

It was raining hard and the wind was whipping the trees. A grinning Nora yelled out, a note of wistfulness in her voice, "Trey and I parked here many times in the summer. Sometimes we'd stay all night in our old van."

When Nora opened the back passenger door and removed Theo from his carrier, Cassie thought she was just checking on him. To her utter shock, Nora, cradling Theo, suddenly ran like a track star toward the back of the market. She grabbed a piece of pipe the wind tossed in her path as she traversed the tangles of decaying leaves and pumpkin roots left in the patch, pushed the pipe in the ground, and sat her son down in front of the pipe. Horrified, Cassie jumped out of the car, intent on rescuing Theo when Nora sprinted back to the car and both heard and then saw a vehicle pull up and park behind the market.

A young man got out and dashed to the back door of the market, unlocking it with keys he pulled from a coat pocket. A woman, equally young, climbed out of the car and stood scanning the area. When she saw what caught her attention she reached into the back seat and pulled out a blanket. She then ran toward a screaming Theo and then to the man. Shortly thereafter, the woman had Theo wrapped in the blanket and sprinted back to the car. The man relocked the market door, got in the driver's side of the vehicle, seemed to check on his two passengers, and then raced out of the parking lot so rapidly that he left behind a large spray of gravel.

Cassie, who felt her blood pressure soaring, turned to Nora and screamed, "Dear God, what have you done?"

Nora calmly said, "Given Theo a chance for a new and happier life."

In that moment, Cassie recalled the conversation she had with Jessica about Nora and she felt hot, stinging rage unlike anything she had experienced in the last 30 years race through her body. "You don't even know who those people are," shouted Cassie.

Cassie saw Nora's lips moving but her words were muffled by the sudden barrage of assorted sirens blasting through the silence that had existed seconds before. Alarmed, Cassie turned on the car radio and instantly heard a male broadcaster announce, "If you're just tuning in, a tornado, totally unprecedented, has struck Principio Furnace in Cecil County. Rescue teams are descending in the area to assess reports that homes and surrounding areas have been destroyed. So far no deaths have been reported. Roads into Principio are restricted to first responders."

"Oh my Lord," Cassie, clutching her chest, said anxiously, "we have to get out of here."

Calmly, Nora instructed her to, "Back out and pause behind the greenhouse. I'll jump out and check the road to see if we can pull out safely."

Reluctantly and wordlessly, Cassie began to back up and stopped when Nora told her to. When Nora stepped out of the car, Cassie imagined her slinking along the wall of the small industrial greenhouse that sat far to the right side of the stand itself.

Minutes later, Cassie saw Nora turn the corner to the car. Opening the passenger door, Nora pulled the seat belt forward to buckle it and then cried out, "Oh no." Reaching in the back seat, Nora pulled out the orange-colored fuzzy monkey.

Nora dropped the stuffed monkey in her lap and

secured her seat belt. Eyeing the stuffy, Cassie said, "Jessica made that."

"The road was free when I checked. Pull out and go right."

Glaring at Nora, Cassie asked, "Where are you taking me?"

"Hospital."

Cassie let out a heavy sigh, "Because you think Theo is there?"

"Yes."

With unbridled furry, Cassie banged a fist on the steering wheel and in a tight voice said, "Nora, I want to be done with this. With you. How dare you abandon your child and involve me in a criminal act!"

Nora said without remorse, "Sorry you feel that way. Theo will be fine. I chose his new family."

"You? You chose his new family?" Cassie demanded. "Have you lost your mind?"

Ignoring Cassie's remarks, Nora told her, "Take the next right. The main entrance to the hospital is ahead on the left."

As Cassie drew closer, Nora called out, "There, in the front row, is the SUV that pulled up behind the market."

Skeptical, Cassie asked, "You know that how?"

"License plate."

Frowning, Cassie said in disbelief, "What?"

"Biddle."

"Biddle?"

"Yes. Jacob Biddle and his wife, Martha. They're being there was providential. I know you're upset and don't understand, but it truly is the best choice for Theo. Trey would agree."

Nora tossed her head back and closed her eyes before continuing. "Cassie, I am so grateful that you and your extended family provided shelter to me and Theo and supported and protected us all these months. I'm begging you to help me complete this journey."

"What journey? You abandoned your son in a pumpkin patch. There's nothing remotely sane about what you've done," snapped Cassie, feeling gobsmacked by Nora's remarks.

"I love Theo. So much that I want a better life for him than I can offer. It's not about money, it's not about his health, safety, and education. I may have birthed him, but I'm not equipped to care for his emotional or his spiritual needs."

Emotionally drained, all Cassie could ask was, "What are you going to do?"

"Give Theo back his monkey."

Cassie just stared at her. "Whatever you intend to do, we first need to find some place to stay. With that radio announcement, we could encounter some difficulty."

"Could you leave me here for an hour?"

Sighing, Cassie said somewhat reluctantly, "Yes. I'll be back in an hour."

Nora tucked the stuffed monkey in her coat and jumped out of the vehicle.

Cassie got lucky and found an old motel that clearly had seen better days on the outskirts of the town that had a single room. By the time she returned to the hospital, Nora was walking through the parking lot to the highway.

She got into the vehicle and snapped the seat belt into the lock. Without looking at Cassie, Nora said, "I wasn't sure you were coming back."

Cassie's response was a snort.

Surprised by the non-verbal response from Cassie, Nora said, "Stuffy is back in Theo's arms."

"How did you manage that?"

"Was standing at reception when both Biddies walked out and stepped directly in front of reception. I asked the woman behind the desk if she knew anyone named Biddle when Martha Biddle stepped up cradling Theo. He saw his stuffy in my hand and started pumping his legs and reaching for the monkey. And no, he wasn't reaching for me. I don't think he recognized me."

"Martha, now joined by Jacob, asked where I found the stuffy and I lied of course and said I spied it near the passenger side of a vehicle with a personalized license plate. The name was Biddle so I came inside to find if someone knew anyone in the hospital named Biddle. Martha believed my explanation, said 'thank you' and took the stuffy and handed it to Theo."

"About the time Martha was thanking me, a doctor stepped out and told her and her husband that the child would be kept overnight for examinations. And then said if there were no problems, they could move forward as a family authorized to foster children. She said she'd personally deliver the boy to them as soon as his medical tests were clear."

Nora and Cassie grabbed subs and drinks from Lindy's Market and then drove back to the motel to discuss their actions for the next day.

"If those tests aren't clear, the hand off may not happen tomorrow," warned Cassie.

Cassie's warning was accurate. After waiting several hours near the house Nora identified as the Biddle residence there was no activity. They returned to the old motel after grabbing more food. By early the next evening, Cassie pulled the old black sedan into a small, wooded area off the side the road not far from the house. It was far too dark for anyone driving by to see who was sitting inside the car.

When an SUV drove by, Nora and Cassie took notice. The vehicle pulled in front of the Biddle house and a tall black woman stepped out and moved to the passenger side of the vehicle.

"That's the doctor from the hospital," Nora said.

Both Jacob and Martha Biddle made a beeline to the vehicle, with Jacob opening the back passenger door and reaching in and removing Theo. Martha collected Theo, who was hugging his stuffy, from Jacob. The doctor handed Jacob a large tote bag and then followed Martha into the house. Jacob closed the car door and brought up the rear.

When the front door closed, Nora, dressed all in black, grabbed the envelope from her lap and walked along the road shrouded in darkness and toward the house. Cassie watched her skulk across the road and move slowly up the stairs to the Biddle porch and drop the envelope onto the porch to the left of the front door. Employing the same stealthy moves, Nora returned to the car pulling off the disposable gloves before securing her seat belt.

"Ready to catch a train?"

"Yes," said Nora with a smile. "Theo is in his new home and about to start a new life."

Cassie pulled onto the road and waited until they were a good distance from the Biddle house before turning on the headlights. Thirty minutes later, she dropped Nora at the train station and said goodbye.

"Drop a line to let me know you reached your destination."

"Thanks for everything, Cassie." Then she turned, pulling the suitcase behind her, and walked into the station.

Cassie sat for a moment, locked the car doors, and then reached in her purse and pulled out her cell phone. Seconds later, Jessica's voice rang out excitedly.

"Cassie, I'm so glad to hear from you. Where are you?"

"Not far from home and I have a story to tell you."

"Can't wait to hear it."

"I may find the nearest motel and wait to make the drive tomorrow."

"Call me when you're about to hit the road in the morning."

"Will do. I'm so anxious to get home."

"And we're so anxious for you to return home."

"Tomorrow, Jess."

16

Blindsided

CASSIE THOUGHT ABOUT RETURNING TO THE motel she shared the night before with Nora and thought better of it. She did an Internet search and found an inexpensive option in Havre de Grace. She pulled out of the train station and headed for the Hatem Memorial Bridge.

A half mile down the road her headlight caught the outline of a truck sitting off the side of the road. As she passed it, the vehicle pulled in behind her with his high beams on. Annoyed by the actions of the driver who she couldn't see, Cassie tapped her brakes twice hoping to get the driver's attention. It didn't work and she was overtaken by raw terror when the car charged like a competitor in a demolition derby, pitching her vehicle forward. Her head struck her windshield and then snapped back.

The pain in her head was intense. Terrified, Cassie hit her brakes and laid on her horn. The attacking car momentarily backed off and then struck her again. She screamed as her vehicle was pushed farther toward an embankment that existed just before the four-lane bridge over the Susquehanna River.

"WALT," HIS WIFE ANN SHOUTED AND grabbed his right arm. "Look at the westbound entrance to the bridge. Do you see what's happening?"

Walt looked and quickly said, "Call 911."

Ann dialed 911 on her cell phone and when the emergency dispatcher answered with the standard "911, what's your emergency?"

Ann responded, "We're traveling east on the Hatem Bridge. A vehicle traveling west on the bridge is being pushed . . . oh my God . . . he just struck the car again. He's pushing the car into the concrete barricade and over the embankment just before the actual bridge."

"Stay on the line; we're dispatching the Maryland State Police," after a pause, the operator said, "Please tell me your name and your home address."

"You're now on speaker phone. I'm Ann Jones and my husband, Walt, is driving."

"Activate your emergency hazard lights, pull over to the far-left lane and stop. Stay where you are until the police arrive."

"Sir, can you describe the vehicle that forced the other one over the embankment?"

"It was big. A big truck. Hard to see because its bright lights were blinding."

"What's that sound? I just heard three loud pops."

"Gun shots. Ann, duck. Pretty sure he fired shots at the car he succeeded in pushing off the road. The driver just pulled a U-turn."

"Mr. Jones, you and your wife need to stay in your car."

"He's getting away, driving the wrong way and dodging some light oncoming traffic. We hear sirens and see three police cars in the distance."

"Mr. Jones, please give me your home address and phone number."

He did, and then a state trooper was standing by his door.

"Mr. Walt Jones?"

"Yes."

"I'm Captain Patricia Armour. Please show me your driver's license. Can you tell me anything about the vehicle you saw pushing the car over the embankment?"

"Not really," and asked his wife, "Ann, did you notice anything."

Ann repeated her husband's words, but added, "The only thing I noticed was that the vehicle didn't have a Maryland license plate."

"No?" said the trooper and handed Walt her business card.

"No," Ann reaffirmed. "When the driver did a U-turn, our headlights caught a portion of his license plate. Is the occupant of the vehicle he forced over the embankment, okay?"

More blaring sirens had everyone looking to the other side of the bridge. A fire engine pulled up, an ambulance right behind it.

"I can't answer that question. Remain in your car." With that, she climbed over the barricade and crossed to the other side.

There was more activity when a responder carrying a bag handed it to Captain Armour. The trooper looked inside and then placed the bag into her car before returning to the Jones vehicle.

"Mr. and Mrs. Jones, thank you for your help. You may get a call asking you to come to headquarters and officially sign a statement of what you did and didn't see."

"We can do that."

"The driver of the car is on the way to the hospital."

"Thank God," the Joneses said in unison.

THE FIRST THING PATRICIA DID AFTER leaving the scene of the crime was to go to the hospital in Perryville and talk with the attending physician. She pulled out a business card to introduced herself at ER reception, asking if it was possible for her to have a word with whoever was attending to the needs of the accident victim that was just brought in.

A nurse stepped forward and took the business card. "Dr. Taylor is in with the patient. I'll give him your business card, Captain, and ask if he can take a moment to speak with you."

"Thank you," said Patricia, then she took a seat in the waiting room.

Moments later the nurse returned saying, "Dr. Taylor will be with you shortly."

Twenty minutes later a bespectacled man of about 50 stepped into the waiting room wearing scrubs under a white lab coat with his name embroidered across the top of the left pocket. Patricia stood, extended her right hand, and introduced herself.

"What can you tell me, Captain, about the unconscious woman, on the exam table?"

"Her driver license identifies her as Cassandra Cooper who resides in Lancaster, Pennsylvania. She's 59 and identified someone as her next of kin on a medical card in her wallet. I'll notify that person of her current condition at the conclusion of our conversation."

Without hesitation, Dr. Taylor described the woman's injuries.

"She's in a medically induced coma. An MIC. Her brain is swelling."

"For how long will she be in that state, Doctor?"

"It varies. I've had patients that came out of a MIC in a day or two, and others who remained in that state for weeks."

"Thank you."

Back at headquarters, Captain Patricia Armour once again checked the contents of the bag recovered from the car driven by Cassandra Cooper. She pulled out the woman's wallet and extracted the medical card she had scanned earlier.

It was 2 a.m., but Patricia made the call.

A male voice answered with a simple hello.

"This is Captain Patricia Armour with the Maryland State Police. Am I speaking with Jeb Cooper?"

A sleepy man asked, "Who is this?"

"Captain Armour, Maryland State Police. Are you Jeb Cooper?"

"Yes. I'm Jeb Cooper. What is this about?"

In the background, Patricia heard a woman ask, "Jeb, what's going on? Did someone forget you're on vacation?"

"Sir, are you related to Cassandra Cooper?"

"Yes. She's my cousin. What's happened?"

Again there was a woman's voice, now clearly upset, "What about Cassie?"

"Earlier this evening, Ms. Cooper was attempting to cross the Hatem Memorial Bridge to Havre de Grace when people traveling in the eastbound lane called 911 and reported a vehicle pushing Ms. Cooper's car over the embankment. Also shots were fired."

Now fully alert and sitting up in bed, Jeb said with a note of authority in this voice, "Captain, I'm Sargent Jeb Cooper with the City of Lancaster Police Bureau. Is Cassie alive?"

"In a medically induced coma at the hospital in Perryville, Maryland. Typically, trauma patients are transported to Baltimore."

"Oh, God. Captain, we have a Level 1 trauma center in Lancaster. We need to arrange to have her transported here. Can you help?"

"Jeb, tell me what's happening. I spoke with Cassie earlier today. She said she was coming home in the morning."

"My wife, Jessica, just told me she spoke with Cassie this morning, who told her she would be home tomorrow . . . today."

"Sargent, let me call Dr. Taylor and ask what arrangements can be made. I'll call you back."

Disconnecting the call, Jeb turned to Jess and said, "Cassie is in a medically induced comma at a hospital in Perryville, Maryland. Someone tried to kill her."

Jumping out of bed, Jess said, "Get dressed, Jeb, we're going to Maryland."

9 780988 933378